E. M. LACEY

ISBN: 978-1-958295-36-6

Edited by: Cynful Monarch

Book Design by: Jessica Cage

Cover Design by: Solidarity Graphics

Autograph Page

Contents

Welcome to Eldritch VIII

This is Blacktooth IX

Names and Pronunciation X

Glossary (In Earthling Terms) XI

Song of Sin XIII

New Teeth XV

Prologue XVIII

1. Wolf at the Door 1
2. Brother to Brother 13
3. Home 24
4. Songga's Prize 31
5. Triage 39
6. A Champion is Chosen 47
7. Time to Move 51
8. A Bitter Truth 54

9. Death of Songga 58
10. A Visit from the Goddess 71
11. The Arms of Luna 75
12. Hell to Pay 82
13. Deadlands 88
14. A Deal She Can't Refuse 97
15. Mentorship 104
16. Father and Daughter 112
17. On the Banks of Elderton 122
18. Luna's Message 128
19. Grace 134
20. Camping with Champions 141
21. House of Testing 150
22. A Seed of Hope & Rebellion 157
23. Echo Chamber 161
24. Have a Heart 175
25. Smoke Signals 189
26. Bitter Words and Bickering Brothers 202
27. Of the Same Mind and Body 211
28. A God's Plan 221
29. What Makes a Monsters 225

30. Alpha Bark 241

31. New Beginnings 251

Stay tuned for "Wild Hunt"!A free short story and extended conclusion to the Song of Sin. 255

Enjoy this Book? Please Leave a Review! 256

Check out more of the Eldritch Trials 257

About the Author 258

Welcome to Eldritch

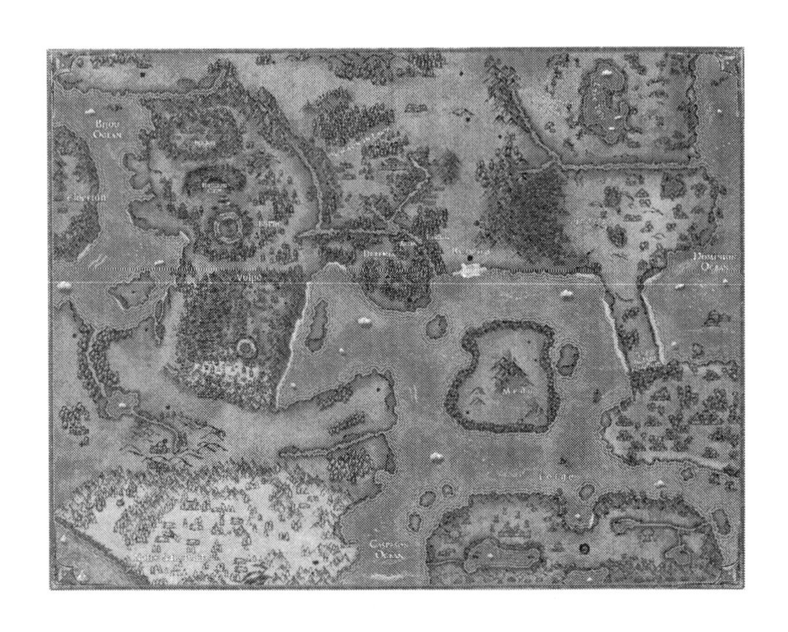

This is Blacktooth

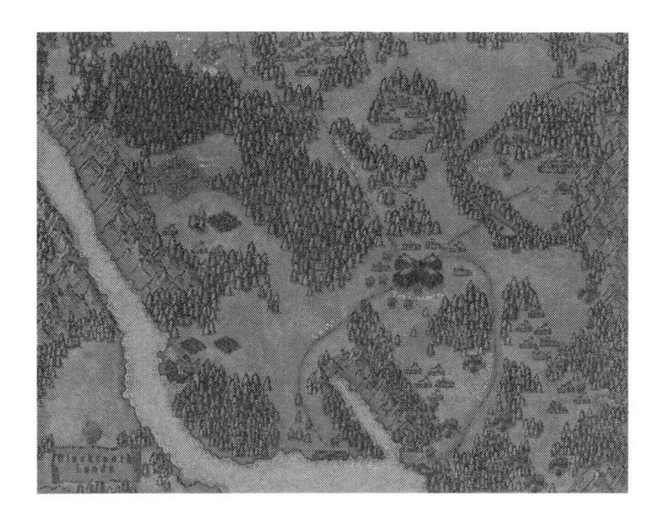

Land of the werewolves. During the story you will learn more about the history of werewolves and why they have been chosen for the Eldritch Trials.

Names and Pronunciation

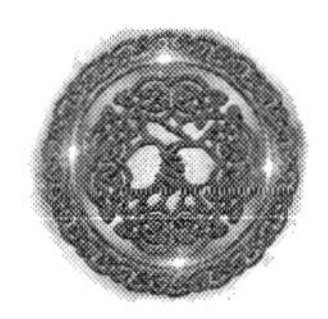

- Mvunaji (moo-vu-nah-gee)
- Adí (a-te) – Navajo word for "big sister"
- Adeezhí (a-dee-zee) little sister
- Dak – dark
- Leigt – light
- Ok'r – Longtooth
- dougan (doo gahn)

Glossary (In Earthling Terms)

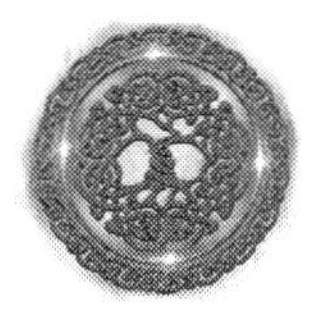

People

- Earthling = Drichians
- People/Person = Eumen /Euman

Common Curse words

- fuck = Jiiq
- shit = shezia
- damn = drakgo
- bitch = fatu
- you hoe= ma hezi
- dumbass= deplu

- ass (asses)= plu (plu’s)
- asshole=pluvuta
- Hello / Goodbye = Hende
- Family = Laenu
- Wehr(s) - used for bipedal beast form

Song of Sin

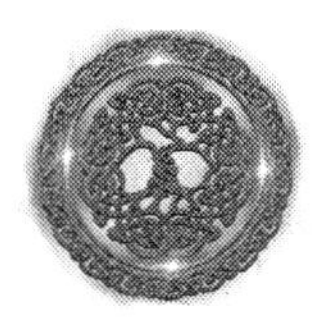

Sin corrupts, but the truth could destroy them all.

The Hasking stone breathes life once more, signaling the Blacktooth pack's time to complete the Eldritch Trials. The problem is they have no champion and limited time to train one. The Alpha's choice is simple - send the wolf who caused their dilemma in the first place.

Rel is no champion and barely a werewolf herself. But thanks to her temper, she is forced to take the role. Rel must enter Elderton and face the House of Testing. If she doesn't, she'll lose the only mother she knows.

The House of Testing is unforgiving and holds no secrets once those doors close. Can Rel handle the truths she discovers about herself? Or the curse she carries that can start a war with a death god.

How will the trials end for Rel and the Blacktooth pack?

A hundred-year curse or war with a god?

Quote from a Cherokee Legend:

There are two wolves, and they are always fighting.
One is darkness and despair, the other light and hope.
Which one wins?

New Teeth

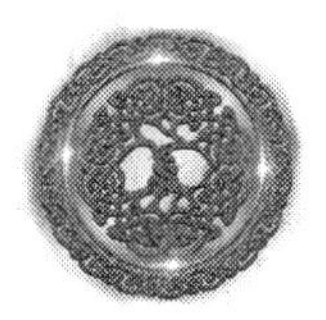

Mgwans cackled as the first seedling in a hundred years broke through the soil in the heart of the Forest of the Black Moon. A curse of them burst into the sky, swirling into a grim funnel that bent over Blacktooth land then broke apart. Far away, on the isle of Elderton, in a house bearing the pack's marker, a young werewolf walked out onto the front step. He stood without fur, eyes closed, a warm grin on his face as he tilted his head toward the sky. The many injuries his mind conjured during The Testing were fading. He stretched his tired body, letting the shift take him. Falling onto all fours, he shook off the remnants of skin. He lifted his muzzle and let loose a howl. In the distance, his pack answered.

The Hasking Stone had already announced his victory to the pack. His father would dispatch a delegation to collect him, but the young wolf would not wait. There was much to be done. The first thing was for him to challenge his father, Chindi. For too long, his father's beliefs degraded the pack's standing. His father believed in shining things like magic, technology, and approval from the Council. Loyalty was a thing of blood, as it was with being alpha. In his father's eyes, an alpha was divine, but Ulmer knew better. His father's ways had broken the teeth of the pack. Brought upon the curse when he failed them.

As Ulmer raced through the maze of homes toward the great gates separating him from the waters of Bijou, he reflected on his pack's condition. Because of his father's greed, he'd earned the wrath of their goddess, Luna. His father's quest to gain a seat at the table of the elders was both futile and destructive. The pack's numbers had dwindled, thanks to the curse. What remained of their kind had become as meek as little foxes who hid among rabbits. Werewolves had become Bleets. The pack used them for meat and fabric. Though Bleets were great woolen beasts with sharp curling horns, they were docile. Capable of destruction but lacking the fire it took to fight.

A growl rumbled in his chest as he plunged into the Bijou. His father brought technology into pack territory. Outside eyes and influence filled the pack with curiosity. Cravings for things not of the land. Rumors spread about his father's pursuit of magic. His desire to bring magic to wolves.

The thought of such things propelled him from the water. He shifted mid leap into his half beast form by the time his feet hit the ground. Large talon-like claws flexed as he considered the absurdity of it. Werewolves were the sons and daughters of Luna. If a wolf desired favor, it should be from Luna alone and not from the pompous beasts and beings on the council.

Their will would have no bearing on the wolves. Not with him as leader.

Ulmer's chest heaved as his decision took root. He ran full speed on two legs as his thoughts burned, weaving the future of the Blacktooth pack. One where werewolves are strong in both mind and body. Their pups would be bred for strength and intellect. All the males would be ready the moment the Hasking Stone burned. The name Blacktooth would fill others with both awe and dread. Werewolves would become feared. Respected. Under his guidance, the Blacktooth would grow new teeth among the populace of Eldritch. None among the others would challenge them. Not even the gods.

Prologue

A Song of Life and Death

She was bleeding again. A thin, jagged trail of blood trickled down her thighs. Argoel grit her teeth against a fresh cramp biting down on her pelvis, but she didn't waver. Her eyes narrowed as she focused on the line of black trees.

She couldn't die, she thought. Not yet. She needed time for her spell to work.

Fatigue washed through her limbs. She tempered her breathing, adjusting her stance for balance. Nausea rolled through her. Dizziness followed. The scent of her own blood mixed with the vibrant wilderness surrounded her.

"No," Argoel whispered. She inhaled. Her mind filled with all the ways she could fail. She exhaled, her breath sliding through the cracks in several teeth. Every inch of her body burned from nearly two years of abuse, as well as the aftermath of childbirth.

"Not yet," she ground out. Her pup's survival depended on her. She forced herself to move. Every step between her pup and the wolves coming for her increased the odds of its survival.

Rotten wood and wild pepper flavored the air.

Magic!

Its smokey green tendrils slithered through the grass. Sparks crackled along its dark edges. Argoel stood in a clearing. Waiting. Bracing herself for magic to strike, but it didn't. It lingered barely an inch from the outlying flora.

Something chuckled. It circled above the canopy of overhanging branches. Another wave of laughter descended through the flapping leaves, placing her on alert. Her eyes darted between the black bark of the surrounding trees. She'd taken a trail considered sacred. The path to the Deadlands, a werewolf burial ground in the heart of the Forest of the Black Moon. She thought superstition would give her enemies pause.

She giggled at her foolishness, or maybe she was going mad. Werewolves had no faith, especially those in the alpha's inner circle. They were dead things. Haunted and obedient to their alpha's will.

Laughter rose again. This time it was closer to the ground, off to her left then ricocheted right before it died again.

"Thought you could escape," a garbled voice descended from the canopy as soft as a leaf. It squawked then burst apart, fading into rolling echoes. She'd heard many voices during her time in captivity, but this one had the quality of a child's.

"You can't get away," a second voice chided, nearly identical to the first speaker.

The phrases repeated, trading places, as they looped and circled relentlessly to weave between the surrounding trees. Close, but not close enough for her to see the speakers. She was tempted to twist toward them, but to do so would give her pursuers an advantage. Instead, she remained, unmoving, at the core of the clearing. Her eyes raised to the darkening sky. Two moons, one silver and one blue, looked down on her. In her heart bloomed a desire to pray, though she'd lost her trust in the gods months after her capturer. Her lips parted, and the words flowed.

"Mother Goddess, guide my hand in this fight." Broken growls littered the air, drifting in her direction. Branches snapped, leaves crunched, and feet thumped across the forest floor. "Don't let me fall." Argoel's whisper resembled a hiss as she reached into her blouse, drawing the stolen blade from a sheath between her breasts. The alpha called it a key. A bright blue dagger with swirling script. It was the only thing that could break the spell that locked away her magic.

"Protect my pup." Argoel hooked two fingers in the space between her skin and the pretty silver collar around her neck. "Place her in the hands of one who will make her strong. Love her." Argoel swallowed the sting of tears she did not dare shed. "Please, goddess." Argoel poured all her hope into her next words. "Luna, take my pup and make her yours. Love her and guide her as such."

Argoel's eyes locked on the dense tree line. She slid the blade against her skin and cut into the silver collar. A soft crack encouraged her to cut faster as the tangle of runes lost their potency. Her nose wrinkled at the acrid scent of death magic. It bit and stung as it died.

A halo of power pushed away from her, incinerating the grass and small bushes as the last link of the spell broke. She inhaled, rejuvenated by her own magic as it eagerly crawled through her veins. The cool sting of it pooled in her throat before settling behind her eyes.

"Luna, grant me the strength to stand against my enemy."

Racing paws merged with growls.

Argoel's lip curled, making room for her lengthening fangs.

"Save me from his hands." Her voice roughened as both bone and muscle thickened and lengthened. Shifting hurt. It always hurt, but she needed the strength of her beast. "I am a daughter of the Deadlands." Crackling realigning joints filled her ears as she let her beast lead.

A lean white werewolf looked down at the thin blade. It seemed inconsequential compared to her thick, talon-like claws. She flipped it, drew back her hand, and waited.

Growls grew in volume, but there was still a little distance between her and the wolves. She frowned, eager for the fight. She cleared her throat, raised her head, and set loose a long baleful song. The distant growling ceased, along with their movement.

She drew in a deep breath and loosed another howl. Her magic twined in its song. It was moments like this that reminded her of the brevity of her power, of what she was.

Her song was a beautiful death knell. She inscribed the hearer's fate within every note. She added to her magic: rage, sorrow, and hope. Not all werewolves were bad. She beseeched the Mother Goddess as her howl ceased.

Death has been my home. May I be welcomed back.

Her prayer rose from the chambers of her heart, as wehrs could not speak. She angled her body, drawing back the blade.

Wise she-wolf of the moons, may I send my enemies to the Deadlands before I fall. Argoel snapped her fully shifted snout. *Tonight, I hunt without my master. Without my pup.*

Argoel was not werewolf but Cŵn Annwn, a death dog. A hound of Gwyl, the god of the Deadlands. She was leaner and faster but just as strong as a werewolf. Maybe stronger. Unlike a werewolf, Argoel could wield magic. Her magic was tied to her home.

The first wave of the alpha's guard came crashing through the bush. Argoel set the blade free. It sailed through the air, finding its home in the forehead of the werewolf leading the charge.

Grant me the time my pup needs.

Argoel growled as she let her beast settle in the forefront of her consciousness. Her euman mind fading.

May my pup finish what I started.

She yipped and surged forward, meeting the werewolves entering the clearing.

Ulmer's general, a one-eyed werewolf, hung back in his wehr form, keeping to the shadows as the others tightened the circle. Something moved to her left. She ducked in time to dodge a dark brown werewolf's swipe of claws. He glided through the unfilled space and smashed into the ground. With his claws, he stopped his roll. He was on his feet and charging at her within seconds. Argoel spun to meet him, aware of the wolves closing in behind her.

Flickering motes of light drifted into the clearing, crackling, and snapping as they did. Her spell was growing. Mwgans cawed overhead. They sensed it, too. Magic. She needed magic to distract them. She decided to use the last weapon in her arsenal, her hound. She relinquished control. Her fear faded as her feral side took the reins, sharpening both her sense of smell and sight. Adrenaline mixed with the crisp scents of the forest. Stark white ears tipped with crimson red fur swiveled.

She lashed out with both fangs and claws, taking great satisfaction in the growing rich coppery aroma seeding the air. Licking her snout, her beast took shape, completing the shift from two-footed were to a four-legged death dog. Her fully shifted form induced fear in those who knew what she was. Dense muscle and bone under a luminous white coat. Her tail, paws, ears, and eyes were blood red.

More werewolves converged on her. Some with weapons, while others charged and nipped at her. It was their way of taunting their prey. Keep harassing until something goes wrong. In the moment of error, the werewolves would fall upon her.

Argoel barked at them. She would be no one's prey. Not anymore.

As Cŵn Annwn, she gained access to her spectral abilities. On four legs, she could move between the natural world and duck into the pockets known to her kind as the slipstreams. It would help her current situation if she did so, but the problem with running a slip stream meant a huge power dump. Her beast was the strongest part of her right now, and she needed every ounce of strength if her pup was going to survive.

Argoel yipped, the click of her teeth forcing the nearest guard back. After her first kill, the others gave her a wide berth, avoiding her claws. Their purpose was to return her to the alpha. He was eager for the child. If it showed an affinity for magic, Ulmer would enslave her pup. Breed it to create an army.

Argoel snarled, crouching low, muscles coiled for the attack. She would fight until her last breath.

A warmth, like a lover's breath, raised the fur along her spine. *Soon*, she thought as she gnashed her teeth and whipped her tail. Soon she would show them what she truly was.

Beating wings set loose a cascade of leaves. Mgwans screeched, "Here!" Its tone rose and fell as it circled a needle bush a few paces away. Several more Mgwans joined the one, drawing her to do a foolish thing. She looked, though it was a quick glance at the place where she hid her pup.

Ominous laughter came before the strike. Three wolves charged her, the first knocking her off her feet.

Argoel drew on the magic she had left, intent on dragging the wolves into the Deadlands. The song of her spell rang in her ears as it began its work, building pressure in her chest, culminating around her heart. Desperate, she grasped the bits docile enough for her to wield and threw them like daggers into the wolves surrounding her, killing two, but the third rolled out of her reach.

If the spell was to do its work, Argoel needed to finish this. Her red eyes locked on her prey, widening, ever so slightly, as she recognized One-Eye.

"Clever fatu," he groused as he stalked her, circling, mindful of her reach. "Escaping the Fist." He jerked his head at their surroundings. "My alpha was right about you." He grinned at her. "You truly are the answer to his vision." He swung his finger away from her toward the needle bush at her back. His smile sharpened.

"That pup is the beginning." His arms dropped abruptly. "And you will be the end."

The twin moons of Luna were losing their balance, as the silver moon began its descent, and the blue one remained. Argoel swallowed, relieving the itch in her throat. Her body felt as if it were being pulled apart at the seams starting with her core. She felt moisture settle in the corner of her eyes.

"No. No. No. No. No." The one-eyed wolf chanted as he crept closer. Argoel matched his pace as she backed away. "The healers will fix you, as they will fix me." One-Eye promised as he got down on all fours, offering his neck as he inched forward.

Argoel growled, willing the spell she cast to quicken. She snapped at him. Driving him back.

The loud screeches of circling Mwgans comforted her as the light of the spell intensified. The scent of burnt flesh were signs of it working.

"I will be Ulmer's end." Argoel's words hovered in the air, bursting like bubbles around them. Her magic allowed her to project her thoughts, making them tangible so others could hear them.

"As mother to the heir of the pack, you will suffer no more." One-Eye made himself as small as he could, his menace gone, as the threat of her loss set in. "As mate to the alpha, you would be matriarch to the pack. Honored and well-kept." One-eye lowered his head enough to seem honorable, but his single eye locked on her, scheming.

She could see it in the flex of his muscles, the subtle press of his arm on his wound.

Send her to safety, Argoel uttered with all her soul, as death magic washed through her, cooling the burn wracking her body. Weariness coaxed her lids to lower, but she kept her focus on the wolf in front of her.

A multitude of white motes, like Dragon's Breath, drifted before her eyes. At first, the colors formed tiny clusters, but when she used her strength to add to the spell, the clusters multiplied, filling her vision with a mix of white, red, and orange.

"No!" One-eye growled as he reached for her. A melody of chimes clattered wildly as the spell finished its work the moment

One-Eye's good arm grasped for her, only to disappear in a cloud of white pollen.

A life for a life. It's what the spell required. The faint haze of her body lingered long enough for One-Eye to see her triumphant smile.

"In time, Ulmer's sin will return to destroy him," Argoel proclaimed.

Argoel's delighted laughter was all that remained, as both she and her pup found freedom.

For Argoel, freedom was death. For her daughter, life far away from the Forest of the Black Moon.

Leaving One-Eye to bay at the emptiness.

Chapter 1
Wolf at the Door

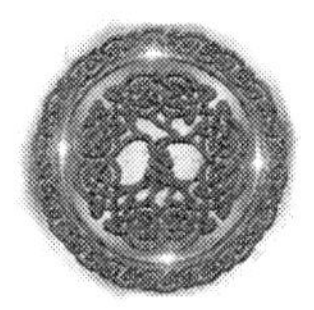

The Hasking Stone breathed, and when it did, the pack bled.

Rel tied off the stitch, grateful she remembered to add the Whisper Oil along the windowsill and the space under the door. It dulled the smell of blood and sickness, which was their only protection from the werewolf lurking outside.

She couldn't believe the mother and pup had lasted as long as they had. A day and a half, stuck in a Cubby with an injured pup. She glanced down at the pup, doing her best to keep her expression hopeful. She would have known they were here if it weren't for her adí, Grace. Her mother, Farah, had sent Grace off to collect medical supplies for her work in the Commons when she came across the distressed pair.

It'd been eighteen days since the Hasking Stone flared brighter than the sun. The moment it burned, all males of fighting age were summoned to the Alpha's Fist to join his adopted sons for the Dominance Fights. There they were pitted against each other. The prize, the winner would become the alpha's successor and champion for the Eldritch Trials.

The thrill of survival did something to the primal mind. It brought on a form of madness to a wolf. Making it feral. A kind of wildness that could only be sated in blood.

The alpha's solution was the Feral Run. Any werewolf, be they pup or elder, caught outside when the Alpha Barked at sunset were considered prey. This was the twenty-fourth year since Ulmer came to power, and the Runs had become commonplace.

No werewolf braved the outdoors when the Alpha Barked. Most locked themselves in by midday. Diligent mothers counted their pups before they locked up their dens.

A hiss of discomfort drew Rel's attention to the task at hand. Her eyes warmed as she offered a smile to the tawny pup curled between his mother's thighs. Alder was a runt and hard of hearing. It was the nature of werewolves to shun the weak, so Alder often retreated to solitary places to play on his own. When the alpha's bark sounded at the brink of Luna's rise, Alder didn't hear.

Rel offered Alder a smile. His eyes flexed. His small bestial hands trembled as he signed. "Are you gonna take my soul?"

"What?" Rel signed back. Her movements were purposeful and slow. "Why would I take your soul?" She pointed at the stitch she'd just finished. "I'm a healer."

The pup's hands steadied as he shook his head and signed, "No. You're Mvunaji, a reaper."

Rel gaped at the pup who gestured at the white blotches on her brown skin. He signed rapidly. "The other wolves say your color is because you escaped the Deadlands. You search out souls so you can get back."

Large gray hands encased Alder's. His mother, Draega, stopped her son's signing with a look of apology on her face. Rel was sure his beliefs came from her.

Rel leaned forward, sniffing softly at the wound. She used the edge of her claw to test her work, checking the tautness of the jagged seam along the pup's side. It would heal well if he remained inside. She applied a light layer of Calendula Paste over the stitches. It would prevent infection and keep the wound numb.

Alder's deep brown eyes tracked her every movement. He did his best to be brave, though no one expected it of him. Alder was barely thirty. Still very young by werewolf standards. He was just beginning to shift small parts of his body. Alder was more animal than euman. He moved about on four legs and in fur. Reason had not formed, only instinct. Rel scratched between his twitching ears, which stilled as she dragged her finger lazily from his head to the mark on the ridge between his forehead and snout. A bold white crescent entwined between a pair of hollow circles. Moons.

All the Blacktooth were born with the mark, all except Rel and her mother, Farah. Rel had a crescent mark on her forehead, edged in red at the ends. A scythe blade on its side, with a full moon cradled between the curve of the scythe. Rel didn't know what it meant. Maybe it was because of her mixed blood?

The werewolf outside clawed and sniffed along the outer wall. Alder's eyes stretched, then watered as his mother's hand compressed on his muzzle.

The Feral Run was near its end. From where Rel sat, she could read the sky. Once the moons sank to half-mast over the Forest of the Black Moon, the Alpha would call back his champions, making the streets safe. Until then, they had to stay quiet.

"Soon," Rel signed. "Soon Luna will give us grace." She sweetened the words with a soft baring of teeth.

A snarl drew all eyes to the source. Scratching intensified, and so did the bitter-sweet musk of fear wafting from Alder.

A thump rattled the window toppling a figurine shaped like a Bleet. It rolled lazily until it reached the edge. Its rounded base dangled but did not fall, but the damage was done. The Whisper Oil concealing their scent smudged. Dull yellow liquid gleamed along the edge of the figurine.

A loud crack ended the moment. All eyes darted to the source as a cloud of wood, dust, and splinters streamed from a growing fissure in the wall. Alder whined, doing his best to make himself smaller.

Rel rolled up her healer's pack, her eyes never leaving the window. She'd already reset all the vials, pouches, and salves to their places. Once she finished, she batted it over to Grace.

Draega tapped Alder's muzzle. There was a rhythm to it. A language between mother and pup. Alder trembled but bowed his head before Draega released his muzzle.

Grace led them away from the wall, deeper into the Cubby. Grace positioned her tiny body in front of them. She swung her healer's pack on her back before drawing a thick stick from a sheath at her waist. Holding it aloft, she gave a brief nod.

Boom!

The side wall bowed and cracked but did not give. Both Rel and Draega took a step back, gazes darting around the room, checking for escape routes when the wall failed.

Boom!

It shuddered, sending a cascade of figurines and splinters crashing to the ground. Another boom, and the wall bowed. A loud crack startled them all. A tuft of dark brown fur pierced through the crack as the wolf pushed against the fresh tear.

Rel signed, "Get ready," to Draega, who nodded in acknowledgement.

Rel bared her teeth as her primal self-scratched beneath her euman skin. Muscles grew taut along the tendons and bone. Her skin burned as her body attempted a shift into something that would never surface. Her mixed blood trapped her beast. It surfaced through her senses, enhancing her hearing, sense of smell, and sight. She had the claws and speed of a wolf but not its full strength. When her beast slumbered, her senses were those of an ordinary euman. But as a euman, she maintained enhanced hearing and speed.

The wall shuddered against the weight of the werewolf crashing into it. Wood splintered. Alder yelped. The wall did not fail.

Another crash created a long fissure which spread from the floor and ended a few inches shy of the ceiling.

Rel faced the breach.

Thick black claws cut through the seam, spreading it wide enough for the wolf to peer inside. It was not normal. Wild magic tousled his fur. Its eyes were unlike any werewolf she had ever seen before. They were different colors like the moons overhead. Its left eye reminded her of the dead. A vacant white orb. The pupil bore the slit of a serpent, while the other was a deep umber. Both its eyes were rabid, darting around for a victim.

Rel danced a few inches shy of its grasping claws. She spared a look over her shoulder. Hands behind her back, she signed. Her adí acknowledged her message with a sharp nod as she moved Draega and Alder until they were flush against the wall.

The wolf spotted Alder and went mad, scratching and biting into the Cubby wall. A sickening snap announced the werewolf's victory as he tore through the wall, taking bits of it with him. Rel wasted no time meeting him at full speed. She dropped so her shoulder connected with his ribcage. The momentum of her charge flipped him, sending him in a spin before his body crashed to the floor. He slid until the wall stopped him, allowing Alder, Draega, and Grace a chance to file out of the hole he created.

Rel rounded on the wolf as it rolled onto its feet. Its pupils expanded. Muzzle drawn back flashing blood-stained fangs. Rel shook her arms, loosening her limbs, before reaching for the sheaths strapped to her outer thighs. Something inside quieted the moment her long fingers curled around the handles of the last thing Rafe gave her. Knives fashioned from Bharg bone in the shape of a fang, only flat. The top of the blades were sharp, and the inner curve was serrated.

Rel led the wolf away from the gap. She needed to buy the others time. It would take them a while to get to the Commons. She hoped they would be safe. The alpha's champion. She slid into a combat stance. Arms out. Knives ready.

He eyed her with malice, but there was a touch of wariness there. Males taking part in the Feral Runs never expected their prey to fight. Especially the females and the pups. Rel's grip tightened on her blades as she hardened her stance. She was a mountain who would not be moved.

The wolf bumped its head against the roof. Cubbies had low ceilings, which did not allow him to rise to his full height. Males in their wehr form were larger than Rel in height and berth. He filled the room, making Rel, who was a sizable female herself, feel small.

He flexed his hand, his claws glinted in the scant light. Peeling back his muzzle, he flashed his fangs. He signed, slowly, making Rel aware that he was far from rabid. There were wolves like him in the pack. They liked to kill. Not for sport. Not out of need.

They killed because they could. They killed to become better at it.

"You ruined my fun," the wolf signed, looking pointedly in the direction in which the others fled. "I like to play with my prey." Vials popped under the weight of his feet as he advanced on her. He made a show of sniffing the air. His lids dropped as if in ecstasy. "Fear," he signed while whipping his tongue around his muzzle, drawing in the blood staining the fur. "It's so sweet."

Rel braced herself for a charge, but the wolf stopped advancing. His measuring gaze swept up and down her body. A slow blink followed by the click of his tongue annoyed her.

He looked down his muzzle at her before he sang, "Why does he favor you?"

Rel blinked up at him. What was he prattling on about? Who favored her? Her nature demanded she seek clarity, but that would require her signing, and she refused to use her hands for anything other than wielding her weapons.

The werewolf smiled an ugly smile as an idea took shape. "I will bring your head to the alpha's favored, as a gift."

Rel backed out of the Cubby, carefully navigating through the debris, knowing the wolf would follow. She needed space to fight, and if she had to, she could run.

He grunted as he shoved his way through. His fur snagged on the frayed edges, forcing him to stop. Rel struck. She charged forward, blades slashing, separating fur and flesh. Her attack forced him to shield his belly, neck, and the large veins in his thighs.

Rel was merciless, severing muscles and tendons, bringing the wolf to his knees. In its haste to escape her attack, more of the wolf's flesh and fur tangled in the teeth of the gap.

Rel ended her attack. Crouched before him, angling her head to look him in his eyes, allowing the thing under her skin to show itself. She snapped big teeth in his face, dropping close to his neck where she nuzzled him, mouth ajar so the sharp ends traced his vein. She felt his grin along the shell of her ear. Rel looked up at the bloody patches of missing fur. He'd freed himself.

He was fast, but Rel was faster. She darted away from his swinging fist. They danced. The wolf swung and swiped. Rel evaded.

He swung his left claw, stopping short to switch to his right. The sudden changeover caught Rel by surprise. His blow sent her crashing face first into the ground. He stomped. Rel rolled. He missed. Rel regained her footing.

His relentless onslaught continued. A glint of steel caught her eye as she spun away from a kick. Somewhere between the wild swings and kicks, he pulled an ax. It was coming in fast, and there was nowhere to go. The wolf charged.

Her skin prickled as glowing orange crackled like lightning licked her body. Spindles of it danced as a disc of the same color spread out behind her. Rel fell into it. The gap sealed as the blade passed through the air where she once stood.

She hit the ground hard when she came out on the other side. The wind knocked from her. She lay still under a large tree, her heart kicking inside her chest.

What just happened? Rel wondered as she rolled onto her stomach. She sat up, looked around hoping to figure out where she was, when a familiar wolf stepped into the moonlight.

Songga sauntered toward her. He was a beautiful terror who towered over most wolves in his euman form. Every part of him screamed power. Sculpted muscles flexed when he moved. Despite his size, he was graceful. A fluid killer.

His russet skin glistened in places where the moon touched. Hair as dark as the night itself billowed like a cloak as he moved. Patches of it shimmered under the fingers of moonlight. He stopped at her side. That was when she smelled it. Blood. It covered him. All of him. Even the sheaths for his blades.

He was naked except for a harness crisscrossing his chest. A series of sheaths held small blades. A pair of long handled double bladed axes arced from their sheaths at his back like grim wings.

"There you are," he said, his grin wide and wondrous. His voice, like the rest of him, was beautiful. Powerful. Primal.

Rel scrambled to her feet, eyeing him as she cautiously backed away.

Songga frowned. "Why are you running away? I was looking for you." He pouted, plucking a small knife from a left sheath over his right pec. "I went to your cottage, and you weren't there." He tossed it up, catching the tip first then the handle. He did this several times as he advanced.

"You're rabid, Songga." Rel sat up. He launched the knife at her, and it sank into the ground beside her with a thunk.

"Not to you, little Mvunaji," he said, pointing to himself. "Oh, what secrets hide inside that skin of yours," he sang, flashing his teeth. "No one knows about those clever little tricks you do." He mimed an explosion. "I will have you."

Dread slithered through her as she considered his desire. The entire pack was aware of Songga's sickness. He was a hollow thing. Females who pursued him didn't live long. He toyed with them. Some he drove insane, and others disappeared.

"We are alike," he said, gesturing between them. "There's something inside you born to murder." He took another step toward her and stopped.

Rel kept her eyes on him but spared a few glances around, searching for a means to get away. She would fight. Her beast wouldn't back down, but with Songga, she wasn't sure she'd win.

As if he read her thoughts, he lowered himself to a crouch. His hands planted firmly on the ground. Head low, but not so low that he could not watch her.

"I allowed the females and the pup their freedom," his tone was neutral as he reached forward, freeing the blade from the ground. "I could have killed them, as I could you, as it is my right during the Feral Run."

Rel swallowed, lip curling at his closeness.

Songga returned to the blade to its sheath, using his proximity to nuzzle her neck. "I would not harm my rightful mate."

Rel shuddered at the idea.

"No," Rel signed.

"You will be my prize," Songga promised. "I will kill whoever I must to make it so." He relented and stepped aside.

"You are free to go, little mate," he said, then slid to his knees before pinning her with his pale gray eyes. "But know this. Any male who comes near you will die."

Rel's breathing quickened as her muscles coiled to prepare for a run.

"Not even the scarred male who tends your land will be safe," Songga promised, his tone cold.

"I will not chase you, Mvunaji," Songga said. Gray eyes tracked her movements but remained still. "But I will come for you by tomorrow's sunset."

A growling snarling beast rounded the corner. It was the wolf from the Cubby!

"Run little mate." Songga chuckled. "I will come for you soon."

Rel took off into the trees as Songga turned to face the charging wolf.

CHAPTER 2 BROTHER TO BROTHER

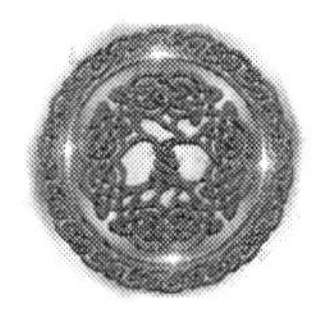

The Mgwan peered up at Rafe with a blue moon at its back. It opened its beak where a small pearl of shimmering light appeared. It pulsed in time with his brother's words.

"The Hasking Stone burns, and the Dominance Fights will begin. Your presence is required in the Hasking Room in two days." The bird paused to pluck a bug foolish enough to crawl across its taloned feet before continuing. "If you are not there when I enter, I will send Songga to collect his prize."

The pearl vanished, and the Mgwan closed its beak. Its head tilted in the odd way of birds. It bowed low before it abruptly took flight.

He growled under his breath as he gathered what he needed for his journey. The alpha's quarters were tucked beside the mountain close to the border gates. It was a full day's walk from Outlands where he currently lived with Farah, Rel, and Grace. It might as well be a weeklong journey with his ailment. Long distance travel was a challenge for him since his return from the House of Testing. Something happened to his brain. The left side of his body was stiff but not frozen. Being a Longtooth had taught him to function through pain. Pain was life, and life was a gift from Luna.

Rafe grunted as he filled a small sack with medicines, water, and the journal he kept. The journal was all he had to offer Ulmer's champion. A collection of nightmares, at least, what he remembered of them. He slung the sack across his body before donning his black cloak. The alpha's mark lined the edges of it. The marks shimmered under the light of Luna's eyes, making his identity clear to his brother's guard. Whether they let him through or challenged him depended on the wolf.

Once he reached the Alpha's Fist, there was a maze to contend with. Inside the maze lurked his brother's guard. Ulmer called them his Fangs. It was their duty to carry out the will of the alpha, which included being dicks to those unfortunate enough to wander onto his territory. It didn't matter if it was pack. One had to be invited, and even that didn't guarantee safe passage.

Rafe flexed his hands. Claws peeked from the nail beds as his mind latched on to wild thoughts of wasted time fighting fools. Part of him craved the fight. It was his right to kill a wolf who dared to block his way. But to engage was time wasted. When his brother called, it would do well for him to answer. Ulmer was not patient, and he was petty.

It would have been easier if he hitched a Bleet to a cart for his journey, but he chose to walk. With the impending Feral Run, his girls would need it. It took Rafe thirty-two hours of travel before he stopped for a night. He took refuge in a Cubby near the Commons. It took another twenty hours to reach the Alpha's Fist.

He entered the mazel, his senses on high alert. Ulmer liked games, and he encouraged his adopted sons to play them. Ulmer's games always involved pain or death. Rafe worked his hands, flexing them to keep them from becoming stiff. His quick pace did him no favors as his muscles protested. He kept going, gnashing his teeth against the shooting pain along his left side. It forced him to put more effort into lifting his left leg. The range of motion was fragile, especially along his knee. He suffered if he bent it too far.

Rafe focused on the elaborate tangle of white stone, manicured flowers, and foliage. It helped his brain to block the pain. The collection of pretty flowers and trees carved by artisans temped those who didn't know better to touch them or lean in for a quick sniff. An innocent act would be one's end, for nothing in the Fist was harmless. Much like the Ulmer, with his slight stature and habit of moving about as a euman. Ulmer, like the Fist, was deadly. Appealing to the eye but deadly to those intimate with it. Rafe stopped in front of the Receiving Chambers. It was carved from black lumber. Magic pulsed inside the engraved wolf's head suspended over a crescent moon. The packs mark fed spells that could paralyze or kill into it.

Ulmer wasn't fond of company, even pack. He believed separation enhanced his position. The pack lands had Ulmer's big and flashy lodge. It was near Gorra Mountain and had golden gates that kept the pack separate from others. Windows stained black with both magic and the skill of the pack's glassmaker kept prying eyes from Ulmer's business.

Being untouchable induced respect. The pack both kin, but they were also his wards. After Ulmer's ascendance to alpha, he restructured the pack. Restored them to the old ways, though his ways had become perverted.

"Hende," Rafe called out.

Hurried steps echoed as they approached. They were light. A female. He stepped back and bowed his head, which caused the hood of his cloak to fall forward, concealing his face. Locks clicked. Magic hissed and popped as it was undone. Dying magic rose like ash. Some of it caught in his nose, bringing on a violent fit of sneezing as the door swung open.

The orange glow of Dragon's Breath washed across the step onto the manicured garden behind him. Magic resurrected, thrumming in the wood. There were a series of enchanted doors, each a different color. Anyone familiar with the alpha's ways understood that each color represented the intensity of the spell embedded in it. Black being lethal. Red guaranteed instant slumber. White meant neutral, but on the other side of every white door lurked Ulmer's Fangs.

"Quickly," the den mother said, ushering him in with the impatient wave of her hand. She was unlike most females under his brother's roof. Though she was slight in stature, her age gave her confidence. The little female stepped forward, grasped his hand, and pressed a square of paper into his palm.

Not sparing him a glance, she stepped away and motioned for him to follow. Rafe knew the inner workings of the alpha's compound well. Heads of prey both wild and wolf decorated the walls between torches and statues of his brother. They took the left hall, which took them to the Hasking Room. There his brother would meet him.

It didn't take them long to reach the Blacktooth's emblem, a wolf's head over a crescent moon. The carving was stained black, but the symbols etched into the crescent moon were deep red. There was no knocker or knob. No magic. It didn't need it because behind the door lay the Hasking Stone.

No werewolf, even those who had gone rabid dared get close to it. To be within its presence was to be near to the goddess Luna. To approach a goddess without consent was to breathe one's last. Offending the goddess meant spending one's afterlife as prey for the god Gwyl and his pack. Gwyl ruled the Deadlands venturing out to hunt the unjust. There were three sides to Gwyl. He offered eternal peace in a lodge of their own. Good hunting and quiet days, while to those of warrior spirit, he invited to hunt with him. For the unjust, once caught, they were stripped of their wolf and forced to exist without a portion of their soul. Forced to exist for the pleasure of the hunt. Gwyl's hunts were never ending.

Rafe swallowed as the little female stood aside and motioned for him to enter. He ducked inside. His heart thumped at the click of the door closing behind him. He never thought he'd see the Hasking Stone so soon. He'd barely made it out of the House of Testing eight years ago. The challenge cycle for the pack had become more frequent. Every five to ten years the Hasking Stone burned. This was the second time since Ulmer's victory.

Rafe lingered at the top step of the Hasking Chambers. The small circular gray stone room was large enough to hold four adult males. Ten steps descended into the chamber. Bench seats were carved from stone which surrounded a clear glass column. In that column was the Hasking Stone. It was mounted on a pilar, nested in crystal rocks. Rafe looked up at the four points holding sonar stones. The image of the Hasking Stone would be projected to the Commons once the Trials started.

The rhythmic pulsing hum of the breathing stone drew Rafe to stand before the crystal column. His hands pressed against it. His own breathing aligned with the Hasking Stone. It shimmered and crackled like kindling as the goddess's power flowed inside. Rafe tilted his head, his ears swiveling in search of its song. A barely noticeable ring, it tinkled like chimes. It was both beautiful and fearsome.

Rafe wondered if Ulmer could still hear it.

A loud clap spun Rafe around. Ulmer stood, dressed in dark red and gold robes. Hands clasped in front of him. Eyes alight as he stared at Rafe.

"Sit, brother." Ulmer gestured toward the bench parallel to him.

Rafe took a spot on the bench opposite his brother.

"We have twelve days before our champion must enter the gates of Elderton." Ulmer launched into preparations for House of Testing.

"The Dominance Fights started later than normal," Rafe stated the obvious. The muscles along the left side of his body ached. He barely made it through his trial, and he had been allotted the full thirty-days of preparation. "How am I supposed to prepare a champion for the House of Testing?"

"My sons are ready." Ulmer gestured at the room's interior, as if the act encompassed the whole of Blacktooth. "My lodge is equipped with training arenas." He thumped his chest. "The den mothers and my Fangs assist in their conditioning. My wolves are ready."

"You know as well as I that physical training alone is not adequate preparation for the House of Testing!" Rafe said. He rose unsteadily to his feet, letting his robe fall open. He slapped his chest which was covered in claw marks. Some were very deep while others were shallow. There were chunks of his flesh that would never grow back. His russet skin was dark in places where his wounds nearly took his life due to infection.

Rafe knew war. He knew battles long before the curse, but the Housing of Testing was like nothing he'd ever experienced.

"I bear the marks of survival, and what good did it do me?" Rafe pointed at the left side of his face which sagged, throwing off the symmetry. The area around his mouth was tight but did not obstruct his ability to speak. He ground that finger into his scalp on the unmarred side. "Here is where the battle rages."

"My champions are tested from youth," Ulmer said, leaning toward his brother, refusing to look up. He imbued his authority into his next words. "I select my Fangs with care."

Rafe returned to the bench, his right leg moving of its own accord, bouncing in an effort to burn off the building anxiety.

Ulmer leaned back, raising his hands as if to placate his brother. "I understand your concern about the mental challenges." Ulmer dragged the word mental, treating it as if it were the start of a joke. "The wolves I raise are strong enough."

Rafe dragged his hands through his hair. The sting along his scalp was a comfort. Ulmer was unreasonable. Ulmer knew what was best, no matter how wrong he was.

"The Dominance Trials have not ended. How many wolves are left," Rafe asked.

"Five," Ulmer said.

"It's been eighteen days, brother?" Rafe asked. "Why did you start so late? There are thirty days from the moment the Hasking Stone lights for the pack to prepare and deliver a champion to Elderton. You know this."

Ulmer grinned and said, "Don't trouble yourself over the details. My wolves are ready." He laid his arms across the top of the bench. "You will have four of the twelve days remaining to share your knowledge with my champion."

Rafe's eyes were wild with frustration. "Four days?" He jabbed a clawed finger toward the chamber's entrance. "Four days to train one of them?"

Rafe leaned back in his seat, exhausted, unaware of the laughter echoing through the chamber as he buried his face in his hands.

"This humors you, brother."

Rafe sobered, realizing he was the source of laughter. "Brother, your wolves are stubborn."

"Survival is a great reward," Ulmer said, toying with the ends of his hair. "They will listen."

Rafe stared at his brother, grateful his warped face cloaked his feelings. The way things were looking, he feared the Blacktooth pack was well on their way to another hundred-year curse.

"The Dominance Fights will end in a night or two. I will give my champion a night to work out his lusts. Once he's sorted, I will send him to you." Ulmer waved a benevolent hand toward Rafe. "I have prepared a set of rooms near the Hasking Chamber. My Fangs will be close in case my champion finds the Feral Run lacking."

"The pack is yours. Your will is done no matter my thoughts." Rafe's gaze drifted toward the Hasking Stone. It was clear. It would remain that way until the pack's champion entered the House of Testing.

"Time, brother." Ulmer grinned. "If there's too much of it between my champion and the House of Testing, doubt will grow. Time can make a strong heart to grow cold." He thumped his chest. "Get weak." His voice took on the rumble of a growl. "Weak wolves fear. Like father."

"Goddess, help us, should a champion lose heart," Rafe groused.

Ulmer leaned forward, pressing the tips of his fingers to the clear glass. His body stiffened as if hit with a current of its power. Ulmer let his wolf ears surface, peaking through his hair above the small flat shell-like euman ones. They flexed toward the glowing stone. The only source of magic he allowed around the pack. A soft smile touched his lips.

"Can you hear it, brother?"

"Yes," Rafe said, his voice was husky.

"I wonder if the Hasking Stone becomes a song to all its champions," Ulmer said. The wistfulness in his tone surprised Rafe.

For a second, Rafe and Ulmer connected, not as brothers, but as survivors. Their eyes met through the stone.

Ulmer rose, his hand still on the glass casing. He pat it lightly. "You will bring your mentee here. Let them see the stone up close."

“I will prepare them in a way I see fit.” Rafe rose unsteadily to his feet. He didn’t like sitting for long stints of time. It hurt his knees and the bit of muscle under it.

Ulmer headed toward the chamber door. “You will introduce them to the Hasking Stone.” Ulmer paused and looked over his shoulder at Rafe, his tone dagger sharp. “Leave him with it.” Ulmer’s fist curled at his side. “The one who enters the House of Testing needs to know what he’s looking for. Know how it feels. Recognize it.”

Ulmer opened the chamber door, beckoning for his brother to follow. “Come, meet the remaining wolves.”

Rafe didn’t argue. He followed his brother out of the Hasking Chamber into the hall. The deeper he went into his brother’s compound a sense of melancholy engulfed him. He missed the family he’d built. Farah and his two adopted daughters. Distance granted them the illusion of peace. Rafe fell for the lie, believing he was outside of his brother’s reach. *There is no such thing as peace for the pack*, he thought as he settled into his room.

Chapter 3
Home

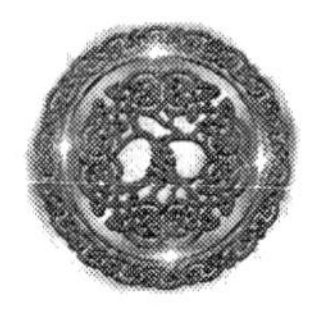

A trail of shimmering red stones guided Rel back to the two-story cottage. Her mother laced their property with several vibrant stones etched with symbols. Rel loved the colors. When she was little, she used to sit in the shadows just to see them glow. Each stone had a purpose. Red stones drove off those with ill intent, while the green beckoned those in need. Rel's favorite were the blue ones. They reminded her of water. It was also like the stone that hung from the silver collar around her neck. Mother Farah called it a Favor Stone.

"The goddess delivered you to me on my saddest day," Mother Farah would say, her face solemn. "It's the day she ended my loneliness." Those words always ended with her mother cupping her face to turn a watery smile her way.

It felt strange walking the trail without her mother. The crunch of leaves mimicked how she felt. Dry. Shattered. So much had slipped away in a single night.

Wings beat overhead, sluicing the canopy. Leaves trickled down reminding her that she wasn't alone. Grace had taken on her avian form and flew overhead. She would stay hidden until Rel gave the sign that it was safe to join her.

It wasn't long before the trees thinned out, giving her a glimpse of home. A small two-story cottage with a water wheel tucked along the side. As she entered the clearing, the scent of moon flowers swelled. There was a bed of them behind the cottage along with an assortment of medicinal herbs. Her mother made her living healing the pack. She also taught those interested in art. It helped that she kept a small herd of Bharg and Bleets. The spiky bovines with their four tusks were mean natured and hard to manage, but Rel had an affinity for them. They also raised Bleets. Large woolly creatures with six curling tusks. Bleets were gentle giants the pack used to pull carts. Their wool was used to make clothes and spin fabric for trade.

The rhythm of her walk changed from crunching leaves to the swish of fine green pebbles under the weight of her steps. The warm orange glow of dragon's breath stored in nets along their territory line mimicked fire. Solid black flowers shaped like the heads of dragons filled harvest nets strapped to stakes. They were blooming. She could tell from the glowing fissures. Motes of pollen rose skyward. Unlike most flowers, they smelled of burnt wood with a hint of decay, making them the perfect guides for the dead. Solemn lanterns, which led the way for mourners to the Offering Plate in the heart of the Forest of the Black Moon. There a dead werewolf would burn. Its ashes would ascend to join the death god, Gwyl, to roam the wild forests. If they were lucky, be chosen as one of his spectral hounds who joined him on a wild hunt, seeking out the rogue dead and those who offend him.

A snap of wings turned Rel around. Grace, the dougan she called little sister, shifted as she descended. Mottled brown wings shimmered, becoming like smoke as they smoothed and stretched until they formed slender arms with delicate fingers the same hue as her wings. Brown legs lengthened, ending in small feet. Her stride fluid from the point of landing to the moment she joined Rel's side at the edge of the cottage gates.

Grace tugged on Rel's half skirt. Large brown eyes stared up from a round purple-blue face. Her euman skin kept the hue of her avian form, though her body was waif-like, much like a water sprite.

"Adí," Grace said.

"Yes, adeezhí." Rel's fingers moved absently, her head turning to look from the dark cottage to the small wooden shack beside the Bleet shelter. She didn't like the emptiness of her home. On a night like this, Rafe would lead the Bleets into their shelter before heading off to patrol their borders.

Another tug. Rel looked down at Grace. "Why didn't we join Mother Farah in the Commons?"

Rel tapped her medicine satchel then signed. "She sent you to me to gather supplies before we got sidetracked with the injured pup." She gestured toward the cottage, signing the word "back". Rel tilted her head, examining the garden a short distance from the water wheel.

Waving her hand toward the Bleet shelter, she said, "Check on the Bleets. Make sure they're watered and fed while I start gathering the medicines."

Grace dipped her head in acknowledgement before darting off to the shelter. Rel braced herself, taking the worn foot path up to the cottage. The stones lining the edge of the footpath lit up with every step. Inside their cottage was the same. Whatever room they occupied lit up. The light appropriate for the time of day. None during the height of daylight. It amplified as the sun set. A simple word, dak, ended the light. While the word, leigt restored them.

Rel stopped in front of the intricately carved red door, unaccustomed to the darkness on the other side. Her hand poised at the knob she didn't turn. Home always made her feel better. She should have felt better, but she didn't. She took a deep breath, opened the door, and stepped inside. The hollowness of her footsteps added to her unease. Glancing over her shoulder at the brightening sky, Rel willed away her discomfort. She had a task to complete. Her mother needed more medicine. More bandages. As much as she and Grace could carry. Standing on the threshold didn't put the supplies in her satchel.

She undid the ties to the satchel as she crossed the threshold. Her pace steady as she passed through the small living area and kitchen to the storeroom door where Mother Farah kept all her medical supplies. A symbol identical to the one on the trees leading to their territory was burned into a placard to the right of the door. Rel placed her hand on it. Her palm vibrated as magic did its work. A lock clicked, and the door to the storeroom swung open. Walls of vials, small bags, and Bharg shoots filled with salves lined the walls. Each item sorted by need. Counter poisons and medicines for serious injuries lined the back wall. Bandages and raw herbs filled two small barrels on either side of a deep blue door. That door led to the laboratory where she and Mother Farah made and packed the medicines.

Rel grabbed what she needed from the shelves closest to her on the right. Making her way around the room, soft clicks of jostling vials filled the emptiness as Rel packed the bag with everything her mother needed. Once she was done, she did a final walk through, inspecting the shelves, making sure she hadn't forgotten anything.

"Adí, I'm done," Grace called.

Rel closed her satchel and left the storeroom. She didn't bother to close the door behind her. It did so on its own. The prickle of magic scratched the exposed parts of her skin as she headed for the front door. The storeroom locked on its own. Whatever spell it harbored; it concealed its presence from others. Only she, Grace, and her mother knew it was there. Not even the Rafe could tell, though the magic at times made his bones ache.

Grace waited over by the Rafe's old place. A small wooden shack with a door he had to duck under to enter. It had a single window, which gave him a clear view of their little cottage. It too was dark. It had been that way since before the Feral Run. Days before they started.

Grace followed Rel's gaze. She tugged on her half skirt.

"Papa will come back," she said as she held Rel's hand. "He's strong. Mother Farah needs us now."

Rel tapped her fist over her heart.

Grace squeezed her hand and tugged. "We have to go."

Rel knew that, but her feet were reluctant. She wasn't a fan of change. The Feral Run disturbed her normal. She could cope with the few days of isolation. She spent them with her family. Mother Farah didn't have to go to the Commons or carry out any of her healing duties in the heart of the Run. Something about the empty buildings on their land bothered her.

Grace tugged again. This time, Rel forced her body to obey. She adjusted the satchel, tightening the straps in preparation for her run. Grace trotted away toward the trail leading away from their home. Rel's weighted steps followed. Grace's run became a leap. She shifted into her avian form, soaring straight up into the air.

Rel clutched the straps tightly, allowing the hidden beast inside to take control. Her sluggish walk quickened to a run. Rel breezed through the forest, shortening the distance between home and the Commons. As her beast carried her farther away from home, part of Rel wondered if she'd ever see it again.

Chapter 4
Songga's Prize

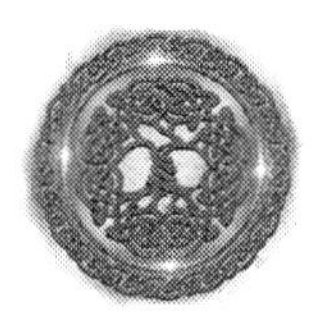

Ulmer led his brother to the receiving room where he would meet the pack's champion. It was a modest space that opened into a garden through a pair of glass double doors. A few trophies were mounted on the wall. The heads of Ulmer's challengers for his place as alpha. Ulmer was always pleased to accept a challenge. He saw it as an opportunity to educate the young and to remind the elders why he was king of their pack. Ulmer was not the tallest nor the strongest among the pack, but he was ruthless. Torture being his favorite vice while murder was his second.

Ulmer made short work of the tour. He had to prepare for the Dominance Fights, which he viewed from an observation suite above the arena behind his home. Inside the suite he kept a series of mirrors. They were from his father's time. Chindi kept a witch at his side. She created devices for his hobbies. She also used her magic to upgrade a series of mirrors that were used for communication within the pack. Before the mirrors, Mgwans were the sole harbingers of communication. The bespelled mirrors were in strategic places within the Commons, mainly the Meeting Rooms and the Greeting Hall. They were a means to broadcast the Dominance Fights. Once those were done, the pack would be able to view the Hasking Stone once the Eldritch Trials began. The remainder of his father's devices Ulmer kept for himself.

Ulmer had some of the bespelled mirrors shaved down to small discs which he implanted in the eyes of several trophies within the Fist. The room he showed his brother had several sets placed at every angle. Rafe was blood, but he learned that kinship did not guarantee loyalty.

They had finished their rounds in the receiving room and stepped into the hall when they heard it. Drops, wet and thick, splashed the floor. Ulmer and Rafe scented the air. Blood! It was coming from the hall adjacent to the receiving room.

Rafe moved in front of his brother and set loose a menacing growl. Ulmer raised the only magic inherent to wolves which was pack magic. The thread of influence wielded by him alone. He coated his tongue with it as he pushed it into his command.

"Come, kneel before your alpha." Ulmer's words pulled at wolves nearby. Rafe trembled before his command but did not bow.

The approaching wolf paused. Blood slashed then morphed into a steady trickle. *Is it a survivor of the Feral Run seeking shelter?* Ulmer wondered as he stepped around his brother, determined to meet the approaching threat. Had prey been herded though the maze?

A steady click of claws joined the splashing.

Rafe flanked his brother, scenting something familiar about the approaching wolf cloaked in the scent of blood and forest. Ulmer's posture relaxed, and his growls died.

Rafe was the first to notice the shadow. The long fluid lines of the shadow evidenced the wolf's knowledge of pack etiquette. All wolves were required to present themselves as euman before Ulmer. It was the Blacktooth way of bearing one's throat to one's better.

Long arms swung in. The end of the right arm was abnormally large. The reason became clear as a severed head came into view.

Rafe growled at the wolf holding it. Songga approached them, naked, except for his weapons harness, which crossed his chest. Each slot held a blade. Arching over his shoulders like macabre wings were his favored weapons, a pair of axes. The one holstered in a sheath on his left shoulder was still wet with gore. In his right hand he carried the head. Ropes of black hair wrapped around his fist, leaving it to swing idly at his side. Fat drops of blood splashed across his legs and the floor.

Songga had never shown an interest in the Dominance Fights, though he'd been raised in the alpha's compound. When he was of age, he moved to Commons taking a job as a smithy's apprentice. He kept to himself, but a young eligible male who refused to participate in Dominance Fights was the topic of all the pack gossip. But it didn't take long to discover his true interests.

Less than a year after his move into the Commons, bodies began to appear around its borders. Always a female. No older than thirty. A time when females experienced their first heat. Since the lifting of the curse, mating and breeding were a priority. Fertile pairs were encouraged to mate. Young females usually found a mate before their first heat. The corpses found around the Commons were torn apart. They were always left in public places, usually along one of the roads. A few were found in the Square.

The Fangs had yet to prove Songga was behind the deeds. Rafe cut his eyes at his brother. He was certain Ulmer was behind the lack of discovery.

Songga stood at a respectful distance from the chamber door. The source of the splashing swung lazily by sodden ropes of hair. The wolf's head belonged to no one Rafe knew. A cursory glance at his brother confirmed Ulmer felt the same.

Both Rafe and Ulmer watched Songga kneel carefully on the blood-spattered floor extending the fist clutching the severed head while canting his own, exposing his neck to Ulmer.

"A gift for my alpha," Songga rumbled as hoisted the head higher. Though he was euman, his voice was still primal. Guttural. Closer to his beast. "An unworthy wolf who dared break the code of the Feral Run." Songga's pale gray eyes darted over to Rafe as his fist tightened in the hair. "He attacked a Cubby."

The wildness in his eyes intensified. “He attacked my prize! Wounded a pup.”

Rafe felt the itch of his wolf’s teeth push against his gums. Its scratching fingers wrapped around his throat, altering his speech as he stared at the dangling head.

“He attacked females and a pup,” Songga said. Fertile females were valuable. For every wolf who died in the fights or the Feral Run, their precious wombs could produce more. Healthy pups were kept safe. Culled from the pack to be raised within the walls of the Alpha’s Fist.

“The pack knows the law.” Ulmer waved at the head. “It was his right to prey upon them since they dared to roam.”

Songga shook his head sharply. “So, we have no need for the healer?”

Ulmer’s brow arched, his eyes flexed, if only a little. His expression remained stoic. “The Feral Run warrants no penalty for those on the prowl.”

“Rel?” Rafe folded his fingers into his palm. The sting of his claws sating his wolf’s need to inflict pain. He hoped it would be long enough for him to figure out the young wolf’s game.

“The words of the alpha state that should a pack member wander outside on the night of a Feral Run, they are prey.” Songga’s fingers tightened in the blood slick hair. “Is not the word of the alpha law?”

Songga tipped his head to the right, his throat vulnerable, but his eyes glinted like the edge of a blade. Rafe noticed the hint of a smile. One he didn’t like.

"Why were you there?" Rafe said, doing his best to remain calm as he questioned the younger wolf. "You speak of law when the rules are for champions to only fight or kill in the arena but not during the run."

"I beg to differ, my elder. It is the right of contestants to bleed or kill to sate their wolves blood lust after a Dominance Fight," Songga said then shook Ize's head. "Be glad I followed Ize. He struck the pup while it was in the open, but its mother got him to shelter. He broke into a Cubby where my chosen attended the pup. He would have killed her when I intervened."

Rafe's eyes narrowed. Songga had taken to calling Rel his chosen since she nearly killed him several months ago. He disrupted a Death March, breaking through the line to snatch the deceased and disappeared into the forest. Rel gave chase. Rafe couldn't figure out how she found him before the others, but when he caught up with them, Rel stood between Songga and the corpse. It took Ulmer's intervention to get Songga to stand down, but Rel was on the winning side of the standoff. She was far from frail, and her temper was legendary. That temper of hers gave her plenty of practice when it came to fighting both genders.

Rafe eyed the head swinging languidly between them.

"The pup, its mother and my chosen are safe," Songga asserted. "Theta, Cahn, Grym, and Atos had already returned to the Den in preparation for fights."

Ulmer folded his arms across his chest, back stiff. His aura swelled, crowding the corridor. It pushed forward, pricking

Rafe's skin. Ulmer's aura spread. It filled the wolves in his presence with what they needed becoming strength for the weak, terror for those who wished to challenge him, and a ring of safety for all within Blacktooth lands. There was something different about Ulmer's aura as the fine hairs on his flesh rose. The nipping of unseen teeth accompanied by an overwhelming heat did not drive him to his knees. Rafe wondered if he was the only one to notice it.

Falling to his knees was hard. It aggravated his stiff muscles burning the broken parts of him. He watched Songga thrust the head forward as he lay on his belly, face to the floor.

"Join the others, Son Songga," Ulmer infused pack magic into his words, knowing it would be hard for the young wolf to move.

"If you will it," Songga ground out, the arm holding the head trembled.

Ulmer flexed his aura, clamping its teeth down on any within range. Several yelps echoed through the halls. Ulmer smirked at the symphony of agony his aura created. He dropped it, satisfied that his pack was thoroughly subdued. He was the big bad wolf after all.

Songga rose, his grip on his prize remained unchanged. Once on his feet, Songga bowed to his alpha.

"Hoist it in the arena along with your other trophies," Ulmer said, waving a dismissive hand toward the young wolf and his prize. "Return to your quarters."

Both Ulmer and Rafe watched Songga saunter away, leaving a trail of bloody footprints in his wake.

Chapter 5
Triage

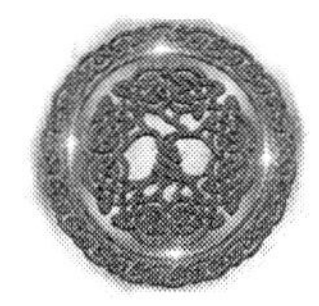

A slender female with pale lavender skin waded through the growing number of wounded. Her white healer's garb billowed like a cloud in her wake as she moved swiftly through the main room of the Commons, twisting her deep purple locks into a braid, which she deftly pinned to the top of her head using the two Bharg spikes clutched between her teeth. The Prime Healer wanted nothing obstructing her ability to tend the wounded. Right now, her purpose was to get the injured settled in a place where they could be aided based on the severity of their injury.

The Commons was a sizable structure with many rooms. A hub of commerce and communion for werewolves. There were three points of entry by way of the Alpha's Spine, Heart, and Soul. Roads aptly named and colored for their purpose. The Spine with its white stone was the common path of travelers and wolves seeking to trade or commune with the pack, while the Soul with its shimmering copper stones guided merchants and their wares to a sorting area where goods were categorized and dispersed among the pack by way of the market. Critical supplies like basic foodstuffs, water, and goods for the seasons were dispensed to all the pack. The alpha took his share first. What remained was sorted by a Den Mother and the appointed Fangs. The Soul was the road which took every wolf to their final journey, into the Arms of Luna where they meet their goddess by fire. Of the three entrances, during the Feral Run, two were locked and barricaded to control who entered. It was at this point, Farah, an elven hybrid, greeted those seeking refuge. She assessed their condition, directing them to a healing station or to a nearby elder. At this point, she also searched for her daughter, who was still out there. Unprotected.

"Help me," a dark-haired female called out as she pushed into the entrance clutching her pup. Big copper eyes scanned the masses. When she spotted Farah, she rushed over.

Farah and her entourage of apprentices spun as if they were of the same mind and body. As a unit, they met up with the she-wolf. Farah immediately began assessing the pup's condition, noting the fresh stiches along his side.

"What is your name, sister?" Farah asked as she pressed lightly along the stitch work for weakness. She leaned in to sniff the wound, subconsciously noting how she'd taken on a few werewolf habits in her two hundred and twenty-seven years of living among them. It didn't escape her notice that the she-wolf did not immediately respond to her question.

"Our master asked you a question," Ashera, a black wolf with a robust voice demanded. Ashera was a large female. Older.

"It is not pack," the she-wolf snapped.

Farah was used to that kind of reaction. She was a hybrid. Mixed blood made purebloods uneasy. "It, being me, is the one from whom you require aid," Farah said, her voice soft, but her words were stern. "Do you not?"

A low whimper forced the she-wolf to swallow her hostility. "I am Draega." She offered up her pup. "This is my son, Alder."

Farah stoked the pup's face. It was warm but not feverish. She had in mind the perfect elixir to prevent infection. There were several salves she could use to speed his healing. The pup wrapped its half-shifted arms around his middle, careful of his injury.

"Do not fret, little one," Farah cooed to the pup, as she stroked his muzzle. "We'll get you fixed up." She scratched between his ears before straightening to address Draega.

"Did you stitch him?" Farah's cool gaze met Draega's.

"No," Draega said, averting her eyes.

"So, a healer gave you aid." Farah glanced at the door behind them.

"It was no healer." The disdain in Draega's tone told Farah all she needed to know, as again, her eyes sought the entrance.

A tug drew Mother Farah to the pup still clutched in Draega's arms. "It was Mvunaji." Cautious hands signed.

Farah graced the pup with a smile. "Is that so, little one?"

"I'm Alder," he signed again, this time his fingers were faster. "The Mvunaji didn't take me to the Deadlands but fixed me up." The rapid fingers stilled then pointed at the neat stitches.

"I'm glad the Mvunaji was there to help you," Farah said as she guided Draega and Alder to a Mending Station. The station was set up for wolves requiring the skill of a stitcher to be tended. Mending Stations were set up in rooms sealed off from the rest of the Commons. She used Whisper Oil to seal off the scents from the rest of the room. Blood and sickness would draw the feral to them. It was her practice to task her apprentices with a purification ritual they believed helped her focus on the art of healing. In truth, the elixirs she prepared were a blend of bitter herbs that hid the traces of magic. It wasn't much, but it did the job.

She rubbed her wrist. Her fingers passed over a thin transparent band encircling it. Her deal with the alpha was to never use magic as long as she lived among them. The band severed her in born magic. Her elf blood allowed her to channel wild magic.

She adapted. It was difficult at first. An euman among werewolves with her pliant skin and thin frame branded her prey. Wolves killed their prey. A frightened wolf needed prey to sooth its beast. Remind it that it was strong. The strong devoured the weak. Though she was not as powerful as a wolf, Farah was far from weak, but her elf blood made her sensitive to wild magic. A thin layer of nature magic flowed below pack lands. It was the same magic that gave Dragon's Breath their fire, darkened the bark of the trees in the Forest of the Black Moon, and caused the moon flowers to bloom. She drew from it to aid in healing, and within the confines of her territory, she used it to encourage the harvest.

Draega lay her pup on a mat and settled down beside him when Ashera drove her away. Farah took her place next to Alder, unrolling a healer's pack. Vials clicked and clacked beside an assortment of different colored pouches. She sorted them, picking up a few to inspect. Draega's protests and promises of harm receded as Ashera pushed her out of the Mending Station into the hall where she would wait while Farah worked.

With her tools laid out for easy access, Farah slid her fingers along the stitching along Alder's side, testing for slack spots. Finding none, she followed up her inspection with the application of gahn root. Gahn root bound to both the stitches and wound. The bond would fade as the wound healed. The fading process thinned the stitches. Once the wound was fully healed, the stitches would vanish.

A tug at her sleeve brought her to face the pup. His eyes wide with worry as gnarled timid fingers signed. "Am I gonna get better?"

Farah leaned in. The pup reminded her so much of Rel when she was little. "The Mvunaji did good work," she said, draping a hand on the pup's middle. "She fixed you so you could travel safely."

Alder looked at the hand draped across his middle before tucking his hands so his mother couldn't see.

"The Mvunaji isn't so scary," the pup confessed.

Mother Farah leaned in. "No, she's not."

A light tap on her shoulder prompted her to take the bowl offered by her apprentice who took their place on the opposite side of the mat. With the help of her apprentice, Farah was able to administer a tea to Alder. Soon after drinking it, he fell asleep.

Mother Farah watched him for a little while, ignoring the growls coming from the waiting area outside. She stroked his face, missing her daughter. Like any mother, her heart filled with worry as she sought the skylight above the room. It helped them keep track of time. Farah frowned at the still dark sky. Rel was out there somewhere. She'd helped the pup and his mother, but at what cost?

Work. She needed to work. Her idle mind would only make her worry more. Rel was strong. She was capable, and a demon looked after her.

Farah swallowed, feeling dirty for such a thought. She busied herself with arranging her healer's pack, but her thoughts wandered to Songga. He was the strongest contender for the Eldritch Trials. It was only the third day, and he'd slaughtered his way from the fifty-four that started to the final five. Songga was obsessed with murder and the pain that came before it, but he wanted Rel. He believed she was his fated mate and proved it in blood. Several males who showed interest were severely beaten. Two died. Most the males in the pack quietly mocked

Rel. The few who dared to do so openly. If Rel hadn't put them down, Songga did.

Shame rose in her again, as her mother's heart found some comfort in Songga's actions. The other part worried for Rel, who woke to the smell of his piss outside her room window. Farah had set repulsion spells around their land to repel wolves of ill intent. Songga endured them. Walked through them, though they burned and cut. She fueled them with the ugly parts of the magic flowing through the land. A tiny part of her believed the piece of magic that drove trespassers away involved the dead.

No matter the pain, Songga still came for her. When he found her, his eyes would swell with the same awe and greed as they had the day he first saw her. It wasn't love. It was an obsession. A need to touch power. A need to possess it. The rumors of her origins didn't help.

Alder shifted on the pallet. Farah nodded to her apprentice, who went off to collect his mother. Draega rushed over, knocking shoulders with her. A subtle twist of her torso knocked the she-wolf off balance, but like a wolf, she dropped to all fours and quickly regained her footing. Draega surged forward, drawing her arm back to strike but stopped short as she felt the sting of a blade against her ribs.

"You move, your pup is an orphan," Farah flashed her teeth. "I've always wanted a son. Alder is sweet."

Draega's gaze followed the path of Farah's hand. The blade rested near bones near her heart. It wouldn't take much to pierce her pelt and puncture her heart. The blade was as thin as a Bharg spike. A Bharg spike would have been worse. The spikes were hollow, which would make her death messy. Draega stepped back and sat beside her child.

"Be grateful you know where your pup is," Farah said. "I'm still waiting for mine." She left the she-wolf and her pup, returning to her vigil beside the main door, taking inventory of all who entered.

Eight hours later, Rel walked into the Greeting Hall with Grace trailing behind her.

Chapter 6
A Champion is Chosen

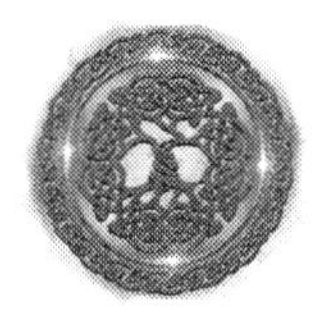

Songga licked the blood from the claws of his shifted hand, savoring the salt of sweat and the sweetness of fear. The red werewolf with a shock of black fur down the middle of his muzzle doubled over clutching his middle. Songga flashed his teeth as his opponent worked to keep his intestines in his gut.

He liked fighting as a euman, shifting only the parts of him for fun. His mouth watered as he sank his short blade into Cahn's shoulder. A purr vibrating along his throat as he sank flat teeth into Cahn's neck. If Songga used his wolf's teeth, the task of tearing flesh would be easy, but easy wasn't his way.

He moaned as blood flowed across his tongue. His eyes sealed, enhancing the taste. His claws sank into the crooks of his victim's arms. He hamstrung his prey seconds before he settled in to torture his prize. The prey's pain sweetened the meat. The pleasure of the kill called to his wolf. It crawled anxiously beneath Songga's skin. He would not let it take over, because when he did, his prize would die swiftly. His wolf would kill then savage the body with efficient fangs and claws.

Songga retracked his claws, smoothing them out to match the soft skin of his body. He liked killing without fur. It heightened the sense of touch. Made it intimate. Skin allowed him to feel the veins, muscles, and bones. He knew which veins brought a quick death and those that bled for days before quietly ending a life. He knew which muscles and nerves delivered optimal pain. Songga knew how to murder with mercy, though he never did. Pain and suffering were his joy. It was his power over those he hunted.

Piss and feces scented the air. His prey was nearing death. Songga grinned, allowing his teeth to sharpen. The wolf beneath him whined. Songga loosened his grip, just a little, allowing his prey the illusion of his benevolence.

The wolf, Cahn, went limp. Songga let him fall to the ground, remaining within reach. Cahn's body convulsed. The remnants of his wolf receded, leaving behind pliable flesh. Songga snorted at the wolf at his feet before he pivoted, giving Cahn his back. He thrust his arms up, his head rising, as he prepared to howl, and as he expected, he felt the prickle of Cahn's shift.

Cahn, a glorious russet wolf, lunged for him. Songga grinned as he went airborne, twisting his body out of Cahn's reach, thrilling at the closeness of his claws. The burn of it slicing into the skin near Songga's ribs. That small tear set free Songga's wolf, a great black beast with white eyes. It was three hands larger than a male Bleet. His wolf instantly met Cahn. Both red and black wolf tore into each other, ripping flesh and fur as they battled. Growls, yips, and the squelch of torn flesh filled the arena. An audience of den mothers and servants watched in silence. It would be their job to remove the loser's corpse and wipe away all signs of the fight.

Songga's wolf, for once, toyed with his prey, prolonging the inevitable before severing the muscle along Cahn's left leg. Cahn's high-pitched shriek fueled Songga's blood lust. His wolf charged the crippled red wolf, latching on to his throat. Songga shook him, his jaws crushing the fine bones in the neck. He locked eyes with Cahn, as life drained from them. It was his favorite part. Taking a life aligned him with the gods.

He dropped the wolf. The life he siphoned from Cahn surged in his chest, fueling his howl, which reverberated throughout the arena. It was his song to the gods. A hymn of dread to the rest of the pack who watched from the safety of their hiding places.

Songga's body flowed from four legs to wehr form without breaking his song. The alpha would set him loose on the pack to play. Once sated, he would begin preparations for the trials. After his victory, the alpha's lie would be tested.

He looked up into the blue crystal hanging over the alpha's seat above the arena. Its glow faded, signifying the alpha was no longer watching.

Songga's howl ceased as he shifted back to his skin. The alpha liked to walk around without fur to show the pack his strength, but his presence among them had lessened since the last trial. Only the wolves residing within the walls of The Fist glimpsed his true self. Ulmer was as blood crazed as Songga, but he used others to sate it. Mind games and assassins were Ulmer's muscle.

"Songga, champion of the Blacktooth pack," Ulmer's voice boomed through the jewel. It pulsed with every word said. "Go forth, sate your lusts under the Eyes of Luna." Bells clanged. Again, the alpha spoke. "In seven days, you journey to Elderton where you will stand for us all."

The clanging bells followed as a naked Songga walked across the blood-soaked arena into the hall. He would show the pack power. He was a much younger and stronger wolf than Ulmer. In touch with his primal side, a side the pack had forgotten.

Songga headed out of the arena, into the maze leading out of the Alpha's Fist. He'd made a promise to the future mate. One he would keep. A promise of suffering to those who would keep her from him. A reminder to her that his way was best.

A feral smile lit his blood-stained face as he cleared the maze. Once free of it, he ran, full speed toward the Commons. He would hunt them one last time. Giving them a taste of what was to come. Unlike the alpha, who murdered in secret, Songga would openly slaughter those opposing him.

Chapter 7
Time to Move

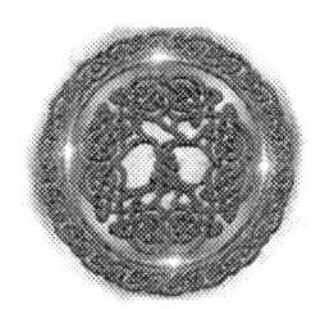

Rel applied her skills to those who would let her. At times, she went out to retrieve the injured, hiding inside the Commons. Some of the pack were too frightened to get aid for their injuries. They had to be coaxed. Some were carried. Her mother would leave no wolf unattended.

"Sihasin," Farah's lyrical voice pulled Rel from her work. "We need make preparations for travel."

Rel nodded.

"Those who can travel without aid will need to leave now. I need you and Ashera to count those who can't so we can prepare."

Rel hopped up to begin her task. She flexed her fingers which throbbed from all the stitching. It was a skill among healers that was difficult to master. Her euman fingers were limber. Rel could thread a Bharg needle with ease. Her hands were not obscured by talon-like claws or a thick pelt of fur which obscured delicate work.

Rel frowned as she tallied the number of wounded. Most were pups, which was unusual. The alpha never allowed the feral to attack the pups. They were the pack's future champions. At least, that was how the alpha put it.

A cacophony of bells trilled, bringing activity in the Commons to a halt. A sizable blue sphere descended from the ceiling in the heart of the Greeting Hall. It pulsed with each ring.

"A time of celebration has arrive," the disembodied voice of their alpha boomed. "Songga, has defeated his challengers. He will take his place as champion of the Blacktooth pack." The jewel's light flared with every word said. "Be honored among the prey, all who fall at his claws and teeth. You are an offering to the goddess. A great privilege." Bells clanged. "In seven days, our pack will again be tested."

The announcement repeated several times before the sphere's glow died, and it ascended back into the ceiling.

Rel could taste the fear in the air. Hearts trembled as every wolf, wounded or able bodied, continued to stare at the place where the sphere vanished. The alpha spoke as if dying was a privilege. Death at the fangs and claws of a sadistic wolf was no joy. The terror etched across the faces of survivors said as much.

This year's Feral Run left many wounded behind. Too many to move to a new hiding place. Rel looked across the room to the large outer windows. Many wolves who frequented the Commons enjoyed them. They offered a grand view of the busy

Square. Many sat at tables to supp, converse, or barter. Now those windows were a vulnerable spot, an opening Songga was sure to use.

Old Elias strode through the room barking orders to those on guard duty as he moved. He headed for the Commerce Hall. Four wolves broke off from the masses and followed.

"It's time to deal with this," he snarled as the five wolves ducked inside a room. They had to do something about Ulmer. It was time to reach out to his brothers.

CHAPTER 8
A BITTER TRUTH

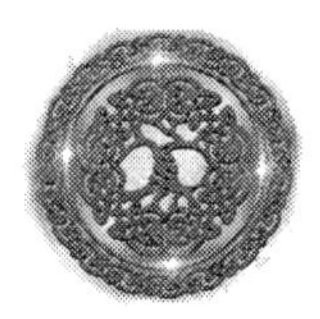

"What the jiiq, Ulmer," Rafe snarled. His unbalanced steps echoed through his brother's suite. Rafe narrowed his eyes as his blood pressure soared. "Be honored among the prey, all who fall at his claws and teeth," he mocked his brother's words. "You are an offering to the goddess? A privilege." Rafe's outrage amplified his voice. His brother was mad. "What's wrong with you?"

Ulmer leaned into his ornate chair. His throne.

"My word is law. I keep the weak outside and the strong close to me," Ulmer said, as he toyed with his hair. "The pack is divided in parts." He leaned forward, using his hands to gesture. "The weak are prey. I used the females to provide sons. The good ones I take."

Rafe's mouth fell open. His stomach roiled. Seclusion had blinded him to his brother's madness. Ulmer continued his lesson.

"The strong I keep here," he said, pointing at the steps under his feet. "I train them." He swung his arms in a wide arc around the room. "I breed the best."

"You kill our own." Rafe met his brother's eyes. There was nothing there. An emptiness.

"I cull the weak," Ulmer spoke slowly.

"Why?" Rafe took a step toward Ulmer. "The weak can be strengthened, but it is your duty as alpha to protect."

Ulmer laughed heartily at that comment. "Like you, brother?"

Rafe's eyes narrowed.

"Who fled the pack after completing the Trials?"

Rafe said nothing as his brother rose from his throne.

"You walked away from us. Away from me!" Ulmer beat his fist against his chest. "It was our time to celebrate. Our time to piss on our father's failure."

"Our father failed," Rafe recognized his part in Ulmer's madness. Ulmer didn't lie when he spoke of Rafe's abandonment. The things he saw. So much madness. There were things so terrible Rafe locked them away in the recesses of his mind, never to think of them again. He studied his brother. Most of those secrets involved Ulmer.

"Our father ran away."

"What?" Rafe snatched his brother by his dreadlocks. He wrapped them around his fist as he glared down at him. "What the jiiq did you say?"

"I saw him." Ulmer's cold glare met his. "I saw him run away before the gates of Elderton even opened."

Rafe released him. He went over to the closest waste bin and threw up.

"You're wrong," he said weakly. "He wouldn't."

Ulmer's went over to Rafe, stooping across from him. "I worshipped father. He brought so much to the pack. He fought hard. Gave the everyone their freedom. So much that many started looking outside our borders."

"I heard some talk of venturing out to Valravn territory. Talks of traversing over to visit the Vulpii or the Aziza Fae," Ulmer mocked the beings, speaking their names as if they were curses. "What would the pack do next?" Ulmer rolled his eyes. "Bring their ways into pack territory?" Ulmer shot to his feet and stomped away. "Thank the goddess our neighbors, the Lyew don't take to strangers."

Ulmer stomped up the steps to his throne and plopped into it, back rigid. "The pack imitates its alpha." He tapped his finger to his chest. "I am not our father." Ulmer growled. "I am not weak, and I will have no parts of it!"

Rafe sat beside the waste bin; hands buried in his hair.

"Our father was a coward," Ulmer hissed. "I will not have his kind in my territory."

Rafe picked up the waste bin and headed for the door. Ulmer stopped him.

"You will do your part, brother, and help Songga as I helped you." Ulmer stabbed his finger at Rafe. "I helped you, though I had no guidance."

"Your one-eyed sycophant was my guide."

Ulmer's expression turned nasty. "I gave him the words because I knew what was to come."

Rafe snatched open the door.

"The House of Testing takes what we most fear, our greatest shame, and throws it in our face. Who would know the shame of Chindi's sons better than me?"

Rafe walked out, slamming the door behind him.

CHAPTER 9
DEATH OF SONGGA

No one expected death to strike at sunrise.

Old Elias and Ashera had moved the pups and their families to a room far away from the Greeting Hall where they anticipated Songga would strike. They were locked in with supplies. Once they young were safe, Old Elias gathered a crew to build a barrier around the Mending Room.

Doing so meant sacrificing the barricade they'd constructed at the main entrance. A few wolves grumbled about it, but they did as they were told. There were no weapons kept in the Commons. Ulmer assigned a rotation of Fangs to patrol the grounds. Theft was rare, as the pack shared their goods. Fighting was the crime that required Fangs. Usually, a random pair of drunken wolves would fight or bickering females.

Old Elias found a few things that could be used for defense. He laid them on one of the few upright tables. A Bharg tusk he pried from a wall. Long blades of wood. He selected the bits with sharp ends. There were a few decorative bottles with sloping necks. He instructed the wolves in his company on their use. After a brief demonstration, he sent them off to their task.

The threat of Songga made him uneasy. He patrolled the Commons, ducking into every room, shepherding stragglers back to the Greeting Hall. Knowing where everyone was made him feel better.

He was on his way to check on the construction of the barrier around the Mending Room when he spotted a tawny pup creeping through the halls. The pup crept around in his wehr form. He was doing a poor job of hiding as he darted awkwardly from the hall to a duck behind a random piece of furniture. He finally ended his sneaking when he pressed against a pillar near the Mending Room.

Old Elias shook his head, recognizing Draega's pup, Alder. His shenanigans would be funny if their situation was not so dire.

"I can see you." Old Elias strode over the column where Alder hid. The pup closed his eyes and remained where he was.

"Oh, for goddess, sake," Old Elias huffed as he stood in front of the pup. "Closing your eyes doesn't make you invisible, you know."

Alder opened an eye. "Aww," he signed.

"Your mother's going to lose her mind." Old Elisa offered the pup his hand.

"But she doesn't like the Mvunaji," Alder complained as they approached the growing barrier. "She said I can't see her once I'm better."

"Rel's a good one," Old Elias said absently as he paused to examine the barricade.

"She's pretty," Alder said wistfully, which earned him a look from the older wolf.

"I guess beauty is in the eye of the beholder," Old Elias exclaimed.

"Yeah," Alder agreed. "She's nice," Alder signed enthusiastically with his good hand. "She's strong."

A silence swept the Great Hall. The fresh smell of urine rose beside him. Old Elias looked down at the trembling pup beside him and followed his gaze.

Songga strode into the Great Hall from the corridor which led to the Alpha's Heart.

"So, you're my rival," he said to Alder as he approached.

Old Elias released the pup's hand, bent, and whispered for him to run, as he brandished the Bharg bone he'd tucked into the waistband of his pants.

His anger spiked when the pup didn't do as he was told.

"Run," he hissed at Alder, keeping his eyes on Songga.

Activity behind him ceased, and someone screamed, "Songga!"

Wolves scattered. Old Elias ignored the chaos unfolding around him. "Finish the barrier," he called out, hoping his order could be heard above the screams.

Songga walked toward him with a cocky grin on his face.

Old Elias trotted forward, raising the bone, hoping the others heard him.

It was the screams that pulled Rel to the gap in the growing barrier.

She'd heard Old Elias' request. *Finish the barrier!*

Rel punched the nearest wolf, repeating Elias' orders. It took a few more well-placed hits and kicks to get the barricade crew working.

Wolves streamed into the narrow gap: two, three, and four at a time. Their bodies knocking against the barrier, threatening its integrity. Rel snarled at them, knocking several down and making short work of the males challenging her. She let her beast show. Its presence drove them back. She forced them into a enter single file as the team tasked with building continued their work.

As they filed in, she noticed Alder. He stood in a puddle staring at the werewolves fighting behind him.

Rel wished she could call out to him. Scream at him to run, but she couldn't. She ran over to fetch him, in awe of the battling raging a few feet away.

Old Elias had Songga on his knees. He slammed the Bharg bone in all the right places, attacking Songga's knees, hands, and got off a few good licks to his shoulders and chest. Songga worked to avoid the old wolf, who held his own.

Rel sidled up to Alder and took his face in her hands to get him to look at her.

"Come with me," she signed. Her presence encouraged the pup to follow.

"No!" Songga roared. He swung his arm, hooking the Bharg bone Old Elias wielded. He grabbed Elias's half arm and pulled, launching the old wolf into the air.

Songga lunged forward, his eyes locked on Alder. "I told you no male could have what's mine," he said through gnashed teeth.

Rel grabbed Alder and leapt out of Songga's way. He skidded to a stop, punching out at the closest wolf. He grabbed the skull of one of the barrier team and squeezed. All the wolves backed away as the wolf had no time to scream. Songga crushed his skull and tossed the body over the barrier.

"I'm coming for you," he taunted as he stalked toward Rel and Alder.

"Move," Songga ordered Rel.

Her eyebrows arched like wings. She stood her ground, shoving Alder behind her.

"She wasn't sure if he would kill her, but she would make him work for her death." She stepped forward.

Alder snapped out of his paralysis, choosing that moment to be brave.

"I'll protect you." The words were mangled by his snout. He moved in front of Rel. The spontaneous move tore his stitches.

Songga trotted forward.

Both euman and wolf were pissed. Rel shoved Alder away, praying that she didn't hurt him too badly.

A wolf as big and as seasoned as him challenging a pup. *What is wrong with him?* Rel thought as all sound faded from her world. She shook her head against her dreadful future. She swallowed. The act amplified the sound of the thundering hearts within the Great Hall. The strongest of them was Songga's. It pulsed with a rabid frenzy.

Their eyes connected as her thoughts pooled, filling her with resolve. She could see his decision the moment he made it. His mouth parted. Her bare foot slid into position, preparing to propel her forward. Her lip curled at the irritating pulse of his jubilant heart. It shouldn't be so strong. It shouldn't be thumping in exhilaration. Songga smirked at her, pausing to wink as he surged forward.

Rel did the same. Her vision washed red as the same orange disc from before materialized in front of the charging wolf. Songga's thumping heart needing to stop its morbid celebration was her greatest desire as she and her beast moved in unison. The orange disc flared as Rel thrust her hand forward, wanting to snatch the offensive organ from his chest. Satisfaction washed through her as fingers plucked his heart from his chest like lon fruit from the vine. She slid to a stop, mesmerized by the thumping organ in the palm of her hand.

Something fell behind her. Rel didn't bother to look. Instead, she gripped the pulsing fruit by its ventricle and held it aloft, oblivious to the blood streaming down her arm as she examined the heart. How could a monster have such a sturdy heart? Songga's possession of one made her wonder if empathy came from the heart or was it a function of the soul?

Rel's brows knit together as she turned it over in between her palms, marveling at its strength. Rel always thought there was a void in the space from which she liberated the organ. Her fingers folded over the pulsating thing and squeezed. It pumped furiously in her palms, like its owner. *Haughty until the end*, she thought as her claws cut into it.

She glanced over at the giant sprawled on the floor. Songga clutched his chest, which was unbroken with disbelief engrained in his face. Rel cocked her head as her mind filled with questions. Why was there no gaping hole in the place where his heart used to be. The only claw marks on his chest were his own.

"Sihasin," Farah screamed.

Curiosity moved Rel to stand over Songga as he died. She crouched, leaned in, and sniffed him. Those wide gray eyes were eclipsed by his pupils. The frantic rhythm of his breathing faltered.

"Sihasin," Farah called out again.

Rel used her free hand to reposition his head so she could look into his eyes. Once it was set as she wished, she untangled the fingers of the hand he used to clutch his chest and pushed it away. As his last breath left his body, she laid his heart on his chest.

"Sihasin!" Farah's voice registered, as did the scrapping chairs and hushed whispers. She stole another look at Songga's corpse. He couldn't prey on the pack anymore.

"Rel," another said. It was Ashera.

Rel looked up and around the room full of watching eyes. The look from her mother drew her to stand. Rel bowed her head in shame but did not regret what she did.

"What have you done?" Farah whispered, cradling her hands over her mouth. Tears streamed down her cheeks. Rel didn't like the way her mother looked at her, as if Rel was a predator.

"She saved us," Ashera asserted, the awe in her voice undeniable.

"We have to get way from here," someone said. Whispers of agreement joined in.

"No," a new chimed in. A matron donning the red and gold robes of a Den Mother joined them. Her sandy brown curls were twisted in a bun atop her head. "We have to get her to safety."

"Rel," Old Elias spoke firmly as he limped over to the protective circle forming around her. His solemn dark eyes fixed on the corpse beside Rel. "The Alpha will come for you."

"What happens with the challenge now?" someone wailed.

"We're going to be cursed," another said.

Mia cleared her throat before speaking. "He was a poor choice of champion," she said before addressing the crowd. "He would have failed."

"Like you know," someone sneered.

"Well, we're jiiqed," a male huffed.

"That's been happening for a long time," Mia said thoughtfully.

"That fatu's killed us all," Draega joined the whining crowd.

"We have until morning," Mia announced, eyes narrowing on Draega. "If you keep this up, you'll bring the Mgwans."

The room went quiet.

Mia turned to Farah. "You and Ashera can seal the room with Whisper Oil."

Farah went into healer mode, running a mental inventory on the ingredients needed to make it. "Ashera, do we have any already made?"

Ashera took a moment to think on it. "We have some."

Grace chimed in, "We have the ingredients to make more."

"Good," Old Elias responded before raising his arms above the crowd. "If you want to save your plu's, or at least buy a little more time, all of you are going to have to work."

Old Elias listened for protests. Ashera gave everyone stink eye, lip curling, daring them to complain.

"Good," Old Elias gave the floor to Farah, pausing briefly as they traded places, alerting her to his need. He pressed half an arm against his ribs.

"What happens now?" Rel signed. "Maybe another male can take his place."

"There are no more challengers," Mia declared, nodding to Farah before she spun Rel away from the crowd. She steered them around the unfinished barricade down an adjoining corridor. They passed through the community kitchen into a storage room. "Songga killed them all." Mia jerked her head toward the door. "I don't think we'll get a champion from that group."

The pack was scared. Rel knew she made it worse. She tugged on Mia's robes. "What happens with the curse?" Rel signed.

"Like I said before, our curse never really ended with Ulmer." Mia plucked a sack from a shelf.

"What happens to my mother?" Rel's hands shook. In her frenzy, she didn't think about her mother. She didn't think of anyone but herself.

"Ulmer will hurt her, but he will not kill her," Mia said, as she examined the contents on the shelves surrounding them.

Rel steadied her hands and signed, "How do you know?"

"Farah is our Prime Healer. She grows the crops that make our medicine. Those crops and the medicines bring the pack a good wage. Ulmer's crazy, but he's not stupid." Mia filled the sack with dried meat and fruit. She added two sleeves of water and a small pouch of medical supplies. "Besides, that fool will be forced to evaluate our numbers. The pack has not prospered since he took over."

Mia held the bag aloft. "No one knows what happens to the pups he takes away. Are the females breeding? Are they even alive?" Mia shrugged. "He doesn't take care of his things."

"The packs isn't a thing," Rel responded.

"For Ulmer, we are." Mia resumed packing, adding a blanket. "Ulmer's will is what matters. It's obvious in how he treats us."

"I didn't mean for others to get hurt." Rel's fingers moved then curled into timid fists.

"If you hadn't done that thing you did, how many would Songga have killed?" Mia grabbed Rel's chin, forcing her to look at her. "The pack is accustomed to abuse. They gripe. They whine, but in the end, they lay down and take it."

Rel sighed.

"Our pack is unhealthy, and if we don't get an alpha who knows how to care for a pack, curse or not, we'll die." Mia didn't mince words. "It's that simple."

She put the bag down then rooted around in the folds of her robes. An a-ha was her song of victory as she pulled a green bag from her pockets.

"These are silons." Mia pressed the bag into Rel's hands. "Use these to get as far away from here as you can."

Mia pressed her lips to Rel's forehead. "If the goddess smiles upon you, you'll find a home with another species."

"I am Blacktooth," Rel stated.

"You're a hybrid. You don't have to claim the pack, just like the pack has never claimed you," Mia said. "Don't feel sorry for us. We'll find a way to make things better." Mia pushed aside the rack she just pilfered. An orange rug slid with it. Mia knelt and threw the rug aside, revealing a trap door. She undid the latch and threw it open.

Several bunches of dragon's breath filled the top shelf of a neighboring rack. Mia liberated a bunch, pulled one out, and stuffed the rest in the sack. She squeezed the stem. It spit pollen as the inner membrane flowed orange.

"Take this." Mia thrust the glowing flower into Rel's hands then pointed to the tunnel below. "Down," she commanded, still holding the sack.

Once Rel reached the bottom, Mia joined her. She swapped with Rel, handing her the sack to reclaim the dragon's breath. Rel followed Mia down the winding tunnel until they reached a dead end, a black upside-down half-moon adorned the wall of dirt.

Mia pressed her right palm to the core of the mark. Pulleys cranked. A loud pop preceded a whoosh of fresh air as the wall swung open to a lush forest. They exited the tunnel. Mia stopped long enough to press something that sealed it. Mia held the dragon's breath high, its glow pushing away the dark. She stopped on a familiar patch of red dirt.

"Be well, Rel," Mia said as she covered Rel's hands with her own. Releasing her, Mia removed one of her many bangles. It was a luminous purple. She slid it on Rel's wrist.

"This will guide you through the forest to wherever you want to go."

Mia backed away. "What happens to you?"

Mia shrugged. "I'm tired, Rel. I am done with the jiiq shezia. Wolves are supposed to bite. Werewolves are supposed be the scourge of the Wilds." Mia tapped a fingernail to her teeth. "Our fangs are dull." Mia squeezed Rel's shoulders. "Don't think that what happens to us is your fault. If anything, you might be what we need."

"How?"

"You showed the pack that monsters can be killed. Knowing they die strips away their menace." Mia embraced her. "Sihasin, start a life somewhere. Your mother will be fine. If you feel the need, return for her once you've made a place for yourself."

Mia headed off into the forest, away from the path she set Rel upon.

Chapter 10
A Visit from the Goddess

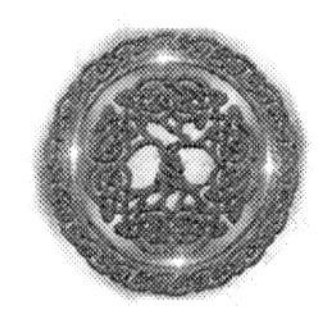

Ulmer lay back, forearms propping him up at an angle, giving him a spectacular view of the moons align. His legs dangled over the edge of the plateau overlooking his home. Blacktooth territory spanned beneath his feet. A tender rumbling in the sky overhead tore him from his thoughts. His chest prickled. He rubbed it. Granular particles of gold drifted from his chest. They winked like starbursts. It was the goddess mark! He'd earned it by completing the Eldritch Trials. He looked down at it, marveling at its glistening beauty. It had not burned since he first received it.

Thoughts of the goddess drew his eyes to the sky. Opaque clouds framed in silver flared as another growl of thunder rattled the heavens. Ulmer straightened, leaning in, setting his elbows on his knees. A silver mist formed between the Eyes of Luna. That mist spread out like a path, and on it, a blue and silver wolf took shape. A beautiful beast. Its fur was silver with a line of blue spiked hairs running along its spine. She trotted down the mist trail, which unfolded with her every step.

Luna! Ulmer's heart sang as he shifted to his four-legged body. He bowed, head down, tail high, as the she-wolf ended her journey to stand before him. Everything inside him wanted to howl with joy. It was rare for the goddess to grace her pups with her presence. He dropped to his belly, pressing his snout between his paws.

"Why have you cursed your people?"

Ulmer raised his head. On four legs, he was much larger than his two-legged euman form.

The she-wolf's snout wrinkled as she bared her teeth. One eye silver. One eye blue. Both burned with intelligence.

"Rise," Luna's voice rang through his head.

Ulmer sat, chest out, eyes feasting on the silver fur before him. He would not dare look Luna in her eyes, though he stole glances whenever he could.

"The Dominance Fights are complete. My champion is at this very moment winding down from the battle." He cast a look off at the Square before returning his eyes to the feet of the she-wolf before him.

The she-wolf's laughter danced along the outer shell of his ears before it echoed in his head, ending abruptly. "Your champion is no more."

Ulmer leapt to his feet. The she-wolf was quick, sinking her teeth into his throat and pinning him. He lay still beneath her teeth. A sense of joy flooded his veins as he relished her touch. She let him go just as his body shivered. Her muzzle peeled back, a flash of teeth, her stance stiff and ready for combat.

Ulmer lay, belly exposed, and his eyes fixed on his goddess.

"Luna, my champion bested the strongest of my wolves. He celebrates."

The she-wolf sat, her ears twitching.

Ulmer listened. He hadn't paid attention to the silence as he sat on the ledge. The argument with his brother busied his mind. His thoughts were loud. So loud that he hadn't noticed the silence. There should be screams. Songga, his champion, was rabid when it came to his blood lust. He enjoyed torture, though he could kill in a variety of ways. Songga was efficient when it came to murder.

"In seven days, your champion is to begin their journey to Elderton," Luna said. Her bell-like laughter followed. The mirth in her eyes chilled as they settled in the quiet. Her blue and silver gaze locked on Ulmer. "As child of the land, you have yet to learn your lesson." The she-wolf pushed up, head high. She looked down her muzzle at him. "Ulmer Blacktooth, you are every bit your father. Only worse." The she-wolf sneered. Her luminous silver fur shimmered. Fine particles of light winked in and out around her body.

She snarled at him before abruptly turning tail to trot into the sky. Her trot became a run. As she built up speed, her very essence broke apart, splintering away into sparkling dust. After a little while, the dust became stars.

Ulmer found himself again ensnared by the beauty of it all. The beauty of his goddess, the singular female he longed to claim as mate.

A howl, weighted by sorrow, broke the spell, turning his attention to the one building with lights ablaze. Strings of Dragon's Breath flickered furiously before going dark. It was at that moment, a female burst through the doors into the Commons. Her arms wrapped around her as she fell to her knees, tossed her head back, and screamed, "Songga's dead!"

Chapter 11
The Arms of Luna

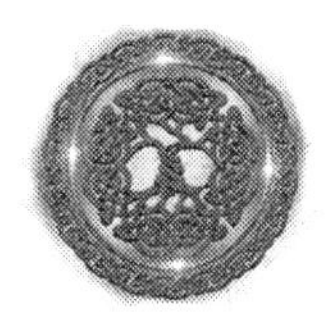

Rel's feet ached. She wasn't sure how long she'd walked, but she would have to stop to rest soon. The red trail only led to one place, the Arms of Luna. She stopped, comparing the trees to the stars. Her mother taught her how to read them.

Count the stars.

Measure the moons.

Is it a half-moon, full moon, or are they both aligned?

Luna's eyes led the way.

Tonight, the skies were clear. Rel examined the stars, searching for a particular constellation. A line of stars with a set of five that formed a hook. It was a marker she used to guide her to the Arms of Luna. Rel positioned herself toward the hook once she discovered it. At its end was the altar. Rel hurried down the trail. Gleaming metallic stone peered through the legs of the trees. She hastened her steps. Her trot become a run. Once she reached the altar, she circled it, examining the surrounding trees. She would use them to get to the top of the altar.

There was no way she was going to spend the sleep on the ground. Not with Ulmer hunting her. He would send the Mgwans to scout, and his Fangs would follow.

Rel walked around the Arms of Luna a final time. The trees on the northeast side of it were the strongest. She went over to them, rearranged her sack, and climbed. She looked across the rippling canopies of dark green, red, and black. She hoped to see Tarac. It was the only place she knew about beings she'd met.

Rel searched for the crop of Dragon's Breth she and her mother tended. It was there she met the Ayinda and Nicanor. They were exiles from Tarac. Using their eviction as an opportunity to explore, Ayinda and Nicanor crossed into Blacktooth territory. Their appearance caught Rel off guard, as with all new things. She found them fascinating, with their arms draped in an array of brown feathers the same color as their skin. Rel had to mind her hands, as she longed to touch the jewels embedded in their foreheads between their antennae. They had hooves and not feet like werewolves or eumen. They had tails that flared like a fish, but they differed in shape and color like the jewels in their foreheads. Where Ayinda's tail was long, ending with a more streamlined fin, Nicanor's flared open like a hand. The Lyew were kind and curious. Her mother warned them to leave Blacktooth territory. Farah and Rel were fine with meeting new beings. They were strange creatures themselves. Werewolves weren't keen on visitors. Ayinda and Nicanor were grateful for the warning and went about their way.

Rel sat down on the altar, fidgeting with the ties of her sack, wondering if the Lyew would allow her to live among them. If they didn't, she hoped to visit the pair she knew. Being explorers, they could give her guidance about where she could go.

She poured the contents of the pack onto the altar. Mia gave her food, water, a blanket, and a bouquet of Dragon's Breath, but there was more. A bundle of paper rolled out, held together by a purple cord. A pen of the same color was neatly tucked inside. A fresh indigo cloak plopped on top of the stationary, followed by three mini satchels. She peeked inside each. One contained three vials of whisper oil, another an assortment of travel medicines, and the last held three crystal orbs.

She took one from the satchel and rolled it between her fingers. It was warm. With each roll, the heat grew. Rel held it up, turning it around, marveling at the building glow inside. A small tear of purple light flickered inside. It broke apart into four rings. On the top and bottom end of the crystal, the rings were small. The two in the middle spread to the edges. She shook it. The perfect coils jiggled, but they did not dissipate.

What is this? Rel thought as held it in her open palm. Each ring flared in succession, becoming blue light. Intricate marks etched onto the surface of the orb. When it was done, she let it fall. Her mother's name pulsed on the orb.

Feeling foolish, she scrambled after it. The little orb took to the air, where it hovered inches from her face.

"Sihasin," her mother's voice called from within. The light pulsed with every inflection.

Rel gasped as she pulled herself backward, widening the gap by a few inches.

The orb spun. Her mother's name seemed to be the thing's face.

"Sihasin," it said again.

Rel rubbed her throat. Her fingers brushing the charms on her collar. The soft gold Favor Stone came to life. It vibrated, tickling her throat.

"What are you?" Soft, raspy words filled her ears.

"My Sihasin," her mother's words bubbled with delight. "I see you've found your voice."

Rel clutched her throat, covering the charms.

"What voice?" the raspy words replied.

The orb drifted closer. Rel flinched. It retreated.

"A gift from your mother," the orb said.

Rel scooted further away, swinging her palms along the altar's surface. She didn't want to fall. The orb was confusing. It spoke with her mother's voice yet... Rel paused, fingering the charms on her collar. That strange raspy noise. It spoke her thoughts!

The orb drifted forward, descending onto the altar. The purple rings from before pushed and expanded, stretching beyond the crystal into a spiraling light. That light congealed into the image of her mother, Farah. It looked at her with stenciled white eyes framed in purple.

Rel scrambled away. Probing hands tipped over the altar's edge, forcing her to stop.

"Sihasin, don't be afraid," the orb said, moving the lips of her mother's replica.

Rel's brows shot up, expression incredulous.

Her spectral mother said, "Gifts from your mother." It waved at the satchel with the remaining orbs.

"Are you a ghost?" the raspy voice asked. Rel's heart thumped as the charm heated.

"I am a message," the replica said. It looked thoughtful, as it considered what to say next. Its stenciled brows rising as its lips twisted in a smile.

"What message?" a raspy response flitted in air like a wisp.

"You must find the Longtooth," the orb waved its arms at the wild expanse. It pointed behind her. Though tempted to follow the path of the pointing finger, Rel kept her eyes locked on the translucent thing.

It pointed at the satchel containing the remaining orbs. "Touch. Find the orb with the red light inside. It will lead you to the Longtooth camp. There, you will get help."

"Help," Rel signed before the raspy noise vocalized her thought.

The spectral replica nodded. "The Longtooth have answers. Seek Ok'r. Speak your father's name, and he will tell you your story."

Rel frowned at the replica's words.

"Find the Longtooth," the replica said again. "Seek Ok'r."

Rel rubbed her head, ruffling her hair.

The replica's expression softened. It gestured to the container of dried fruit. "Eat." It waved a hand toward the blanket. "Sleep."

The mere mentioning of the word triggered Rel's fatigue. Her muscles reminded her of their hard work. Burning. Aching.

"Eat. Sleep. You have a long journey ahead of you," the replica said. "Ask me your questions once you've settled in Longtooth territory." The replica burst into particles of white and purple light. That light flowed into the orb. It flickered. The light inside it died, but her mother's name remained on its face.

Rel reached for it but did not pick it up, afraid it would resurrect. Using the blanket to roll the orb back into the little satchel, she put it in the bag. For now, she needed to prepare for the night. She shook out the blanket and folded it into a pallet. Her empty stomach rumbled, reminding her she needed to eat. Pulling out fruit and a sleeve of water, she placed them next to her blanket. With the night's meal prepared, she liberated a fresh Dragon's Breath from the bunch and separated the parts she needed and stored the rest for later.

It didn't take her long to get a light started. She had no need for raw fire. Fruit didn't need to be cooked. She used some of the water to wash away specks of blood staining her skin. Rel chewed on the dried fruit as her mind digested the replica's message.

The Longtooth.

Her father had told her many stories about them. He was one of them. A warrior from the wild time of the werewolf. The Longtooth withdrew from the pack in the first year of Ulmer's rule. They seemed immune to pack magic or had the will to ignore his call. Longtooth were shrouded in rumors. Some were good, but most were terrifying.

Rel finished her meal, pulled out a vial of Whisper Oil, and slathered it all over herself. There was no way to conceal noise out in the open, but the oil would conceal her scent from any hunting party the alpha sent after her. Once she was done with the Whisper Oil, she doused the dragon's breath with a little water. It didn't take much to kill their glow. She lay down on the pallet. Sleep claimed her swiftly, oblivious to the shrill scream in the distance, confessing her sin to the night.

Chapter 12
Hell to Pay

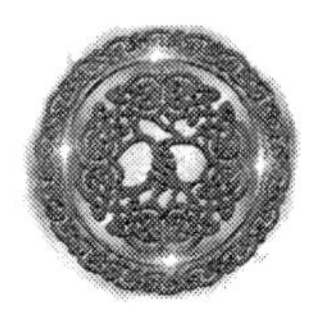

Ulmer's Fangs descended on the Commons hours after the sun rose, dressed in Bharg hide armor stained red with the blazing blue and silver mark of the alpha over their hearts. The pack offered no resistance. They had taken down their barricades and sat waiting in scattered clusters throughout the Great Hall. Songga's morbid shell lay before them, curling in front of a kneeling Elias. He held his head high, eyes defiant, as he offered his neck to the one-eyed guard striding in.

"Elias," One-Eye boomed, as if he were greeting an old friend. "Why are you always the source of trouble?"

Old Elias didn't respond as the wolf stopped in front of him.

"It was the Prime Healer's pet!" Draega cried as she raced from the incomplete barricade sealing off the Meeting Hall. She dropped to a crawl as she got closer.

"Ungrateful fatu," Ashera hissed when Draega crawled by. Ashera was ten paces behind Old Elias. She used her size to shield the pups and young mothers cowering nearby.

Draega stiffened, pausing long enough to reply. "What she did will kill us all." Draega searched the room for allies. Heads turned away. Many turned their backs. "Jiiq all of you."

Draega crawled beside Old Elias, knowing he could do and say nothing while they were in the audience of the Fangs.

"I am Ho'yee." The one-eyed wolf lay his hand under the alpha's mark and inclined his head. "Speak, daughter." He glared at the others. "Your confession will spare the innocent." Ho'yee looked down on Draega, humored by her blossoming hope.

"It was Rel," she spat the name, still furious that she had to submit to her. She held her tongue at the Cubby for Alder. He was all she had.

Draega had birthed four pups before him, but they were strong. The alpha claimed them all. She had no mate to make more. Thanks to Alder's flaws, she could keep him. She didn't mind the whispers and looks of pity. No more did she worry about late night visits or displaying him out in the open.

A tiny part of her was grateful to Rel for saving him, but she would not sacrifice him again. Not when she didn't have to.

"Go on," Ho'yee encouraged.

"She murdered him," Draega said, her accusing glare flaying the old wolf beside her. "To protect this old fool."

Ho'yee clucked his tongue at Elias. "Trouble," he grunted.

"I don't know why she jumped into a fight that wasn't hers." Draega sneered. "But she did that." She jerked her chin at the withering shell curled in front of them. Rigor stiffened his limbs.

Ho'yee circled the corpse, frowning. He stopped, resting a foot on Songga's body and lifting his gaze to Draega.

"How did she do this?" Ho'yee dropped beside Songga, running his hand across the shoulders, then around to the chest. The congealed blood framing the body boasted a large wound. He waved over two of his guards. Together, they rolled Songga over.

The skin sunk over the left side of his chest. The space above the heart. Songga's russet skin bore a deep red stain in the concave over his heart.

"How did she do this?" Ho'yee asked again. This time, dropping the pretense of kindness. His guard grabbed Draega, slamming her down beside Songga. One rubbed her face in the blood.

Ho'yee grinned, appreciating the theatrics.

"I don't know," Draega whined. "I don't know!"

Ho'yee bared his teeth as he glared at the masses. "What did she do?" His voice took on the growl of his beast.

Their silence rankled.

"How did a female rip the heart from a warrior's chest without breaking the skin!" Ho'yee shifted to his wehr form as his voice rolled through the room. He pressed his foot on Draega's back. His Fangs shifted to their wehr forms. Several remained euman. It was their duty to announce the pack's punishment.

A young wolf stepped forward. His tawny fur and umber eyes were familiar to Draega.

"Bring the Prime Healer," he called. A dark brown were shifted from two legs to four. The large brown beast pressed his nose to the ground as he dashed off to carry out Ho'yee's command. He disappeared behind an incomplete wall of broken furniture. There were screams. There was no struggle. Moments after he vanished, he emerged with his prize.

Every eye followed Farah and the dark brown wolf as they emerged from Meeting Hall. Farah stood before Ho'yee. The dark brown wolf rejoined the Fangs, who had fanned out, blocking the exits. There was a Fang stationed at the mouth at every corridor, effectively confining the pack in the Greeting Room.

An euman with dark gray skin stepped forward and said, "It seems your status has made you arrogant, Prime Healer." Squaring his shoulders, he marched back and forth before Farah, eyes narrowed. "Though your skills benefit the pack, you've forgotten your place."

Ho'yee snatched her up by her left arm. The dark brown wolf knocked Old Elias down, pinning him as he attempted to intervene.

Farah dangled, suspended in Ho'yee grasp. She did not struggle.

Her surrender infuriated Ho'yee. Pressing his muzzle to her nose, he snarled.

Farah looked on, resolved and blinking as Ho'yee's saliva trickled down her face.

"Ungrateful." The dark gray euman stopped his marching.

Ho'yee sank his teeth into Farah's hand, and she screamed. His wolf grunted, satisfied with her pain. He added all his weight to the foot pressed against Draega's back. The sticky sweet scent of fear soared as he yanked his foot out of her back. He let Farah hang from his muzzle for a little while before he let her drop.

Ho'yee circled her to make sure she was properly cowed.

The alpha would not approve his harming of the Prime Healer. Ho'yee surveyed the damage. He didn't shake the female, though his wolf wanted to. Farah could heal herself using a talent few knew she possessed.

He walked away from her, fully shifted into a euman by the time he reached his Fangs. Doing an about face, he stared down at the terrified pack. Dragging his arm across his bloody face, he flashed stained red teeth.

"You will lose a third of your number today as penance," Ho'yee declared. "Bring the hybrid and the crippled wolf to the alpha," he said. His expression warmed as the smell of piss melded with fear.

It is good for them to be afraid, he thought as he strode through the band of warriors before him. They parted as he passed.

"Remember the alpha's mercy," Ho'yee threw over his shoulder, not breaking his stride. "He spares both fatu and pup." He tossed up his hand in a dismissive wave, triggering the murder of a quarter of the pack's number. The alpha commanded the slaughter of the elders, males first. Females were more manageable. Many would be spared.

He looked up at the lip of the mountain hanging over the alpha's home. A brown wolf rose, tossed its head up, and howled. Ho'yee let the shift take him and joined his alpha's song. Whispers of rebellion were rising. Bloodshed was the only way he knew to end it. Hurt the weak. Kill their hope. Rebellions died.

Ho'yee stopped to take a final look at the Commons. His gaze drifting up to the sun. A bird, probably one of the alpha's Mgwans, soared above the rising screams. It headed east toward the Arms of Luna. Maybe it was a minion of Gwyl, scouting for souls to bring to its master. Ho'yee chuckled at the thought as he resumed his trek into the Alpha's Fist. The rebellion was as good as over. The capture of Farah's daughter was the only thing left.

CHAPTER 13
DEADLANDS

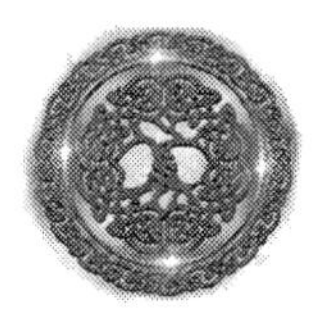

"Adí," someone whispered repeatedly.

Rel's head jerked back and forth as her body rocked. Small hands shook her until her eyes fluttered open. She stretched her aching body. Fatigue clung to her as she curled back into a ball on her pallet.

"Adi," the urgency in Grace's voice woke her.

"Adeezhí," Rel signed.

"They're coming," Grace hissed, as her head swung north, south, east, and west as she continued urging Rel to move. It was what she said next that moved Rel to rise. "They hurt Mother Farah."

Rel pulled Grace into her arms, hugging her tightly as she cried. "They hurt Mother Farah," she whispered repeatedly.

Grace sat back, using her bare arms to wipe away her tears, her slight weight resting on Rel's thighs.

Rel tapped her shoulder, her hands moving slowly as she asked, "What happened? Where is she?"

Grace shrugged, fresh tears building as her little chest swelled with sorrow.

"What happened?" Rel asked again.

"Ho'yee."

Rel waited, expecting the story to flow, but it didn't.

Grace's mouth opened and closed several times before more words came. "Ho'yee. He came for Mother Farah," she said, arms flailing about. "He hurt so many." Grace's tone was grim as those flailing arms landed with a slap to her sides.

Rel relaxed her grip, hoping it would prompt Grace to continue her story.

"What happened to Mother?" Rel asked, brows rising with her question. Her hands hovering at her chin.

"Alder's mom said you killed the bad wolf." Grace's chest heaved. "She told Ho'yee."

Rel's hand opened like a flower, then she pulled it back, sealing her fingertips tight.

"Ho'yee said Mother Farah was ungrateful, and he bit her hand." Grace mimicked the act of biting. Her teeth clicked as her lips pushed up in a sneer. "Ho'yee promised bad things for the pack." Grace's dark eyes met Rel's crimson orbs. "He's coming to get you."

Rel's wrists curled as fingers danced. "I have to keep running." Rel looked off across the forest. Somewhere out there, the Longtooth had a camp. Her mother's replica said they would help her. Maybe she could get them to help the pack.

Leaves crunched underfoot toward the Alpha's Soul. The same red trail that guided her to the altar. Rel removed Grace from her lap, then crawled on her belly to look over the edge. Ulmer's Fangs approached from the crimson trail, but others advanced from the west side. It was easy to see them from her vantage point.

Their bodies carved a clear path as they shoved at branches and stomped on leaves. Rel pulled away from the edge, moving to the center on top of the etching of Luna. The wolves circled the altar.

"Didn't Bren say he heard she was coming here?" a wolf below asked. His voice drifted back and forth below.

Another chuckled. "You sure he told you the truth, Mal? You did nearly break his arm."

Silence hung between the pair below. A chorus of militant steps converged below the altar. They pooled on every side.

"They say the healer's daughter is from the Deadlands," one of the new wolves said. His voice was soft thunder.

"Maybe that's how she did that thing to Songga," a younger male exclaimed, his tone still pitched high. "They say she walked through him like a ghost."

A smack ricocheted along the base of the altar.

"Stop," a new wolf joined them. "Those mutts in the Commons startle at their own shadow. What's that old saying? 'Fear finds monsters everywhere.'"

“Monster or not,” Mal replied. “Bringing her back alive is what the alpha wants.”

“What do you think he’s going to do?” the young male asked. His high-pitched voice squeaked.

Rel could feel the shrug.

“That’s not our business, Prye,” Mal replied. “The four of you can guard each point of the altar while the rest of us fan out.”

“She’s gotta be here somewhere,” Pyre grumbled. “We can’t go back without her.”

“Don’t worry about time, Pyre.” Mal moved south of the altar. “Ho’yee’s sending reinforcements.”

“Going to need wings to find her in all this,” Pyre groused. “Either that or one of you gonna climb up that altar.”

Rel’s heart lurched.

“Jiiq that,” Several wolves said in unison.

“I might do unreasonable things on the order of our alpha but climb that,” a wolf off to the east said. “Dying is much simpler.”

“How does that make any sense, Dax?” Pyre asked.

“It’s like this. You offend the goddess; you’ll be plu out in the Deadlands. I don’t want to spend my eternity being tracked and murdered on repeat. I mean, I only know maybe ten or twelve ways to kill. Gwyl knows more. He’ll make sure I experience all of them.” Dax walked east. “I’ll take my chances out here.” His voice grew distance. “If I’m lucky, a Longtooth will get me.”

Rel inched closer to the edge, leaning to get a better view. A chestnut wolf sat, ears twitching as it scanned the shadows. Something skittered in the distance. The chestnut rose halfway, poised to dash into the undergrowth. A dark gray wolf chuffed at the chestnut. He carefully returned to his sentry posture. Paws down, chest out, ears on swivel.

Rel crawled around the altar, checking on the wolves below. All donned their wolves. Ears and noses twitching at every trembling leaf, bush, and skittering critter. Rel was confident none of them would venture up to the face of the altar. Deathwalkers used poles to raise a wolf to its place on the altar. Her mother taught Rel how to climb. It was her practice to walk ahead of the families, reciting the rites of Luna, then Gwyl. She made the offerings. Prepared the body for its journey. When the grievers arrived, her mother was already on top of the altar.

Rel rarely took part in the Death Sojourns. Her mother was adamant that she didn't, choosing to take her along to harvest Dragon's Breath and tend to the altar. They polished the stone, trimmed back the trees, and kept the space free of weeds. During Muda, Rel was forbidden to go into the Forest of the Black Moon. Muda was a holy day. On holy days, the spirits of the dead roamed.

A snap of wings nearly squeezed a scream from her. She spun toward the noise. Seeing nothing but the vast dark framed by an array of trees, Rel laid her hand over her heart, hoping it calmed. The wolves below could hear it.

More flapping wings. Branches of the trees at her back trembled. Leaves rubbed together. Something scratched and pecked at the bark of the tree.

Rel squeezed her eyes to slits, turning to inspect the shadows. The scratching continued. Small claws digging through the wood.

The scratching, digging claws ended abruptly.

Click. Click. Click.

Tiny tapping claws scratched.

Click. Click. Click.

Tiny tapping claws moved closer.

Click. Click. Click.

The gleam of bone pushed from the darkness.

Click. Click. Click.

A Mgwan hopped into the moonlight. It's head moving the way birds did, stopping inches away from Rel and Grace. It pecked at the altar before looking at the two. Its head tilted left, right, then up. Black eyes stared into her.

Its beak opened. A pearl of light swirled inside.

Rel felt her life leave her body when the Mgwan's message played.

"You've done a bad thing," Ulmer taunted. *"I've lost a champion."*

The Mgwan pecked the altar. Nipping its claws before it opened its beak and continued the message.

"What are you going to do to fix that, Rel?" Her mother groaned in the background. Someone called her mother a

name. Blamed her for their suffering. Spitting and curses framed Farah's moans. *"Your mother needs you."*

"Don't–" Farah began. She squeaked and was silent.

Ulmer chuckled. A teasing, pompous chanting. *"There is no honor in sacrifice, daughter. At least, not for a single person. Honor the pack in your return. I have an offer that will return your mother to you."* Ulmer paused briefly before continuing his message. *"Your mother lives if you are back in my receiving room. Be there by the next sunrise, and I will restore your mother to you."*

Ulmer hummed. *"I might even allow that deformed dog...I mean Old Elias, to live."*

Rel wrapped her arms around her stomach and squeezed. She hoped it would calm the bubbling in her stomach. Bile climbed from her gut and lingered in her throat. Lifting her head, she continued to rub her throat in a downward motion, fingers knocking against the Favor Stone, hoping to quell the rising sickness.

"I know you're up there," Ho'yee called from below.

Rel vomited. Pulling her legs tight against her chest, she locked her arms around them, bending her head until it rested on her knees.

"Our generous alpha has made an offer; will you save the healer and the old dog? Or will you let them die?"

Rel rocked as she considered Mia's request. She told her to run and not look back. It would be best for her mother if Rel built a new life. One in which she could welcome Farah and Grace.

“Are you going to run, or will you kill more of the pack with your insolence?”

“Adi,” Grace whispered as she rubbed Rel’s shoulders. Grace shooed away the Mgwan with the stomp of her feet and several false charges. She wanted to kill it, but it wouldn’t change anything. Mgwans were tools. “Adi.” Grace squeezed her big sister at the shoulder.

Rel stopped rocking, unfurling like a flower as she locked eyes with her little sister.

“Protect our mother, Grace,” Rel’s hands gestured slowly.

Grace nodded.

“Go find her,” Rel continued. “She’s in his dungeon.” It was the only place he could put her. Rel did not know where it was. She wasn’t sure if anyone outside a few Fangs knew. But Grace had a homing instinct. She imprinted on her mother and Rel when she was just a toddler. Rel saved her from a Bharg who played catch by tossing her around with its horns. Her mother nursed her back to health. Grace became family. She could find them no matter where they were.

Rel rubbed her gut. Mind made up. She crawled over to her bag and pulled out the satchel with the crystal orbs. She walked on her knees over to Grace and pressed the bag into her hands.

“Go.” She flicked her hand at Grace. “Give this to our mother.”

Grace lingered, bouncing from foot to foot as she bit her lip.

Rel flicked her hand again. “I won’t be around to look after her for now. I need you to take care of our mother.”

Grace bent down, using the satchel's tie to secure it to her left ankle, moving into a runner's stance, then sprinting away. With every step, her shift progressed. When Graced reached the end of the altar, her wings flapped, and she took to the air. Sailing into tree and shadow before she soared high, breaking through the canopy a short distance away.

Rel watched her until Ho'yee called out to her again.

"What say you, Mvunaji?"

Rel walked over to the northeast side of the altar, speeding up for the leap. Landing in the nearby tree, she shimmied down. Ho'yee sauntered up. His guards flanked him.

"Mvunaji," he taunted. "Killer of champions." Ho'yee snapped his fingers. A pair of guards closet to her grabbed her arms, tying them in front of her. "You will make amends for what you've done," Ho'yee promised as the others spread out.

The pair assigned to Rel prepared for the journey ahead. An euman with light brown skin shifted into a tawny wolf. He bowed. The other had picked her up and put her on the tawny wolf's back.

"Hold on to his fur," the wolf said and pressed Rel's hands into the fur around the neck.

Rel held on as the Fangs surrounding her did what she couldn't. They melted into their wolves. Yipping and prancing. Ho'yee was the last to shift. He let loose a long baying howl. At its end, he sprinted down the red trail leading back to the Commons. One by one, the others followed.

Chapter 14
A Deal She Can't Refuse

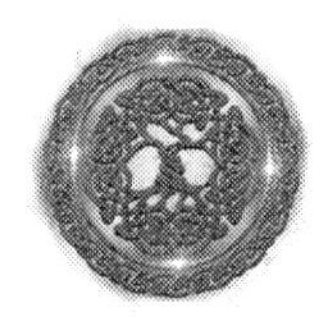

They crossed into the maze in a little over five hours. By the time they cleared it, Ulmer stood outside the Receiving Chambers.

"Welcome, killer of champions!" Ulmer spread his arms wide in mock celebration as the tawny wolf Rel rode deposited her on the front step.

Rel stretched. Her legs were stiff from the ride. Ulmer gestured excitedly for her to come in. She followed. Her pace was cautious as she took in the overdone interior. Trophies hung in a neat row along the wall. Some were the heads of beasts while others were euman. There were a few creatures that were preserved. Whole bodies posed like statues she'd never seen before. Things with withered skin. Some blue. Some were green, while others were black. The creatures had the look of a dragon but were too small. Their facial features were also off. The lips, slick and slimy, brought to mind images of a fish. There was no hair on the bodies.

"Don't dally," Ho'yee snapped.

Rel faced forward while checking out her surroundings with darting glances. They traveled through a series of long corridors with jagged turns. The alpha's lodge had many parts. Before visitors were granted access to the rest of the alpha's property, they had to pass through a receiving room for testing. She detected magic. It wreaked of spoiled meat and blood. Whoever laid it did a poor job of masking its presence. Subtle dips in the walls and along the floors were the marker of well-laid traps, at least to the incautious. Though she'd never been inside the Alpha's Fist, she knew enough to be on high alert. Ulmer was not benevolent. It was a lifesaving practice to examine every step. Be careful where you lay your hand.

A covered pathway connected everything within the borders of Ulmer's compound. The group moved from section to section, padding through the Den Mother's quarters first, which fed into the dorms. The dorms housed Ulmer's adopted sons. Beside it was the training rooms. Tucked in the middle of the three buildings was a grand dining area with an equally grand kitchen. It was empty now. The Dominance Trials were done. Rel wondered if Ulmer would start them up again, this time with her as a competitor.

The group pushed past the arena, ending at a bulkhead door which sat a short distance away. Ho'yee and another guard jogged ahead of them, undid the locks, and removed a thick chain, then opened the doors. A subdued amber light coated the walls. Ulmer walked over to her and took her hand. Rel was noticeably taller than Ulmer, whose head crested slightly above her elbow.

Rel followed docilely. She hoped her submission would improve her mother's odds of survival. They descended a spiral staircase framed by a brick wall. Mounted railings fashioned from black lumber aided their descent. The staircase opened into a galley with three connecting corridors. A thick metal door secured each corridor. The galley was well lit. Rel looked up. A glass dome covered it. Amber glass muted the sun's brightness, keeping the space cool.

Keys clinked in sync with Ho'yee's steps as he went to the door parallel to the stairwell. After he pulled it open, Rel and the alpha entered. Ho'yee passed the keys off to another wolf and followed them. They descended another set of stairs. No twists, but a straight descent of twelve steps. At the bottom, the gallery did not flare into a languid space. This secondary gallery formed a tight square which broke off into a single hall. It felt boundless, though there were an even number of eight cells on both sides.

Ulmer released her hand, gesturing to a cell at the end. As Rel got closer, she noticed the hall bent into a tight corridor which led to another set of stairs.

"Healer," Ulmer called out, his voice jovial. "I brought you a surprise."

A groan answered the alpha's call.

Rel hurried over to the cell. Her mother lay on her side atop a pile of straw, cradling left hand to her chest. The bandages were sloppily applied, giving it a messy and uneven look. If the wrapping was clumsy, how well had her assigned healer cleaned the wound? Were the correct medications used to treat it properly?

Her mother's lavender gaze brightened when she spotted Rel. Her lips pulled back, exposing her teeth. They chattered. Signs of a rising fever.

Rel pressed her head against the bars and gestured. "Has anyone treated her?"

Ulmer frowned as if disappointed. "I did the bandages myself." He stood next to Rel, making a show of examining his patient from afar. "I have done a fine job for a novice, don't you think?"

Rel squeezed the bars, then let them go. "What is your will, alpha?" She looked over at Ulmer, who seemed enthralled by his handy work.

"You will be the pack's champion."

Rel's eyes stretched. She expected punishment, but not this. Her as a competitor had to be a cruel joke. Females did not compete. Not only was it the alpha's will, but in their history, all the champions were male.

Rel's hands exploded into a flurry of gestures.

Ulmer scowled. His hand shot forward, grasping Rel's Favor Stone. "We're not doing that." Ulmer mocked Rel's signing. He rubbed his thumb across the face of her Favor Stone. It gleamed.

He pointed at the stone. "Who gave you this?"

Rel jerked her head toward her mother.

"Figures," Ulmer said, still holding Rel's Favor Stone captive between his thumb and index finger. "Did she ever show you how to use this?"

Ulmer released the charm.

Rel shook her head. She had no idea what her Favor Stone was capable of before her night in the Arms of Luna. She thought the spectral copy of her mother was a dream. It was easier for her to accept.

"Farah," Ulmer called. Farah, still on the floor, swung her torso in their direction.

Ulmer lifted the Favor Stone. "Make it work." He released it.

Farah pushed up, then dragged herself over to the bars using her good arm. She lay on her back, stretched out her right hand, taking the charm between two fingers, and pressed down.

"Let your words find a voice through this stone," her mother said.

The soft gold Favor Stone came to life. It vibrated, tickling her throat. Rel wrapped her hands around her neck.

"What is this?" Rel's disembodied voice flitted around her head.

"That's more like it," he said. He snatched up Farah's injured hand. Rel lunged but didn't get far. Ho'yee caged her in his brawny arms. Ulmer unwrapped Farah's hand. Once freed, he held out his hand. Ho'yee added a blade to it.

Rel struggled against Ho'yee's grip as the Ulmer laid the blade over her mother's pinky. Rel stopped struggling and listened.

"Now that I have your full attention." He pressed it into the finger. It bled a little, but the cut was not deep. "This is what's at stake." He pressed harder. "I will take a finger for everyday you are in the trial. From the moment you leave for Elderton to the time you clear the House of Testing. I will take a finger until you return."

The blade of the knife glinted in the light as Ulmer brought it down, but he stopped just short of breaking the skin. "If you don't make it," Ulmer began, "Your mother will not die," he promised, "but I will make her hurt."

He flipped the knife, aiming the butt at Rel. "You, my dear, will be exiled immediately."

"Yes, alpha." Rel's disembodied voice startled her.

"Good." Ulmer returned the knife to Ho'yee. "Now that we understand each other. I'm giving you three days to train before you are sent off to Elderton."

"What?" Rel's disembodied shook the bars. Dust trickled from the arch.

Ulmer pressed a finger to his temple and tapped. "The only thing we have time to prepare you for is the mental." He gave her an appraising look. "Fingers crossed that the House of Testing doesn't hit you with physical challenges."

Rel felt the arguments surface. They trilled in her head, flickering and scratching, eager to be free, but she held her tongue. She focused on the flickering, scratching sensation. She hummed, distracting her brain, until the flickering, scratching sensation in her head stopped.

Rel agreed, and Ho'yee released her.

"What now?" Rel rubbed her arms.

"You meet your mentor," he said. "Ho'yee will take you to your room." He stooped beside the cell, waving his hand between her mother and himself. "I've gotta discuss some things with your mother." He waved them away. "I'll join you soon."

Rel wasn't happy with leaving her mother alone with Ulmer, but she obeyed. Fighting would cause more trouble. Rel followed Ho'yee from the cell, up two sets of stairs, to exit through the bulkhead door. He left her in the Den Mother's quarters where she waited to meet her mentor.

Chapter 15
Mentorship

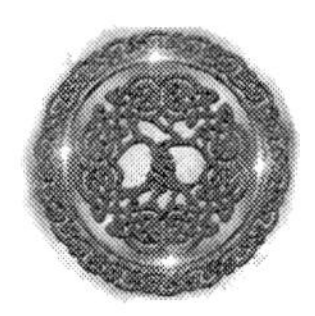

Rel was escorted to the Den Mother's quarters where she was left to wait for Ulmer. While she waited, she toured her room. It was modest with modest furnishings and a large bath. There were no clothes in the drawers or closets, limiting Rel's wardrobe to what she had on. She pulled the hem of her shirt to her nose and jerked away. She would bathe as soon as Ulmer was done torturing her with his company.

After touring her temporary room, she pulled up a chair and waited since there was nothing more to do. She wasn't allowed to explore the Alpha's Fist. Not even the neighboring dorms or the arena. Ho'yee informed her that her meals would be delivered by a den mother. If she needed to stretch her legs, Ho'yee would escort her in area's preapproved by Ulmer. Her freedom was limited to the mentor's quarters and the garden flanking it.

Rel rocked in her chair as she wondered what training would be like. The Dominance Fights were brutal, and Feral Runs were worse. She held no curiosity when it came to them. As a female, she would never compete. At least, it was the expectation. Males were the champions in Ulmer's crusades. Females were mothers, healers, and toys. Every wolf had a purpose. Rel was unsure of murder's role in the pack hierarchy.

Why was murder the only way for a champion to prove himself? Murder accomplished what? Rel leaned forward, holding up her hands. Inspecting them. She'd murdered. Her palms throbbed in remembrance of the heart that pulsed between them. They flexed, resurrecting the feel of the organ. The taut muscle was limber enough to pump blood though the body. She buried her face in her hands. Would she face real monsters in the House of Testing with real fangs and claws?

Her grim musings were interrupted by a knock. She walked to the door and pulled it open. Her eyes bulged as they feasted on her visitor. Rafe filled the doorway. His expression mirrored hers.

"Daughter," he exclaimed, arms spreading open to embrace her. Rel backed away.

"Why are you here?" Her disembodied voice siphoned the exuberance from him. Rafe's arms descended as he bent his knees carefully to get a closer look at the glowing charm on her collar.

"I can ask the same of you," Rafe said as he reached for her Favor Stone. "Why are you here?" Rel jerked away, but his long right arm caught her and pinned her as he took up the charm between the thumb and index fingers of his left.

"Say something," he insisted, his fingers pressing on the stone.

"Why did you leave?" The Favor Stone heated, but it didn't burn.

Fascination lit his eyes, which tracked Rel's omniscient voice as it hovered then popped like bubbles. He'd always wondered what she would sound like. Her words held Farah's accent. Rel folded her hand over his.

"Why did you leave us?" she asked a second time.

"The Eldritch Trials are upon us, and it's my duty to prepare our champion as best I can." Rafe plucked at his cloak.

"But you were not a champion." Rel shook her head sharply as she did the math. "The last trial was nearly fifteen years ago." She released his hand, backing away to look up at him. Rafe made her feel small. Not in a bad way. A father was always larger than everything in his daughter's life. "You came to us from the Wilds. You lived with us for twelve years."

"My brother runs away," Ulmer said as he came up behind Rafe. "He leaves everyone."

They stood side by side. Rel looked from one to the other. She didn't care for Ulmer. Her capture and mocking were her first exposure to him. Rumors of the alpha were plentiful. None flattered him. No one ever spoke of his looks.

The brothers were the same deep tan skin. It was the hue as cured Bharg leather. The eye color was different. Rafe's were a dark gray that bordered on black while Ulmer's were an even umber tone. Both wolves were powerfully built. Ulmer, though compact, didn't lack muscle. Those umber eyes were always assessing his surroundings and the wolves in his company. Her father's face sloped lower on the left side, but the right half was like Ulmer's.

"Brothers." Rel tasted the word. Not on her tongue but weighed it in her head. Twelve years of boundless affection. Her father never once spoke of a life before her mother, Grace, and herself. His first two years were silent. He carried out his chores: tending the Bleets and Bharg. At night, he disappeared into the Wilds. Rel caught glimpses of his predatory nature when he patrolled. His eyes assessed everything. When he patrolled, his wolf took over. It was upright, absent of her father's deformity. At night, with his wolf leading, her father was a bigger version of Ulmer.

"Yes, brothers," Ulmer said, pushing into the room. "Our family has participated in the trials for three decades." He hooked Rel's arm, spinning her around and leading her inside. Rafe trailed them.

Ulmer gestured toward the bed. Rel sat while Ulmer grabbed a chair and took a seat in front of her. "Our line has championed the pack." He rubbed his hands together. "First our father, Chindi." Ulmer pressed a finger to his chest, "Then me." He waved dramatically toward his brother. "Rafe completed the last trial."

Ulmer leaned back in his chair, legs splayed, as Rafe settled beside her on the bed. He reached for her hand, but Rel pulled away. He did not try it again.

"Songga was to be our champion for this upcoming trial, but he died." Ulmer shrugged. "So, now you're taking his place. And he," Ulmer pointed at his brother, "is going to prepare you for the mind games ahead."

"But I haven't trained for the fighting part." Rel looked between the brothers.

"Fighting is how I test for strength." Ulmer closed his legs, clasped his hands together as if to worship, and lay the tips to his chin. "Dominance Fights show me how predatory my wolves are." He leaned in. "In a fight to the death, one's mind must be quick, adaptable, and always working out the end game. It's not just about the blood and death."

Rel considered what he said. It made sense in a way when it came to the ways of killers. Her father taught her those skills on their land. He did it without blood and punishment. Tending Bharg and Bleet forced her to adjust her approach. She knew how to exert her authority, wear it like a shield as she moved around with the moody swine. They respected her boldness and responded to gentle words after they tested her, while Bleets required reassurance. Rel was the protector when she worked with them. Calming them in the face of storms. Chasing away both beast and objects they found intimidating. Nurturing livestock did the same thing as Dominance Fights. Rel opened her mouth to share her thoughts but decided against it. Ulmer didn't seem like the kind to listen if what was said wasn't in line with something he already decided.

"My brother here will begin your training after you bathe and eat." Ulmer wrinkled his nose.

"But I don't have..." Rel began. The door flew open. Three females entered dressed in red and gold robes. They carried clothes, toiletries, and a tray of food. The group worked silently as Ulmer watched. They were efficient as they stocked the drawers, closet, and bathroom. Ulmer didn't speak again until they left.

"My ways may be cruel, but I take care of what's mine," he said. He got up and left the room, leaving her with her father.

"How did you end up here?" Rafe prodded. He resumed plucking the edges of his cloak. It gave his eyes a place to look since Rel wasn't comfortable with him at the moment.

"I did what he said." Rel wrung her hands in her lap. "I killed Songga."

Songga's death was a mercy, Rafe thought. That wolf was a stain on the pack. He frowned at Rel's fidgeting. She was a fighter not a killer. Wolves were brutal beasts who only understood pain. Rafe taught Rel how to hurt her opponents. Rel made it her conviction, applying her knowledge efficiently in battle. Broken bones, dislocated limbs, and plenty of bruising. They were her brand. Many carried her brand. It made Rafe proud, but murder was its own beast.

Murder was a ravenous dog that could never get its fill. It left a mark on the soul that did not go away. He'd been numb to it for years when he fought in his father's wars. After he dropped his first ten bodies, he became numb to it. It wasn't until he stopped that the dead came for him. They followed him through every chamber of the trials. Accusing. Biting. Always seeking parts of him.

He glanced at her, his pride as a father swelled. She wasn't his seed, but she was a child of his spirit. Knowing her quieted his spirit. Teaching her how to walk among wolves taught him how to deal with his demons.

He reached for her hand again. She let him fold his over hers.

"What happens now?" Rel leaned on him, head resting against his shoulder. Rafe draped his arm around her shoulder and squeezed.

"I teach you how to survive." Rafe rubbed her shoulder. "It's going to be hard."

"I know," she replied, reaching across her body to squeeze the hand on her shoulder. "Lately, everything's been hard."

"At least your mother's safe." Rafe's breath was warm on her scalp.

"She's not."

"What?" Rafe's soothing ministrations ceased.

"Mother's not okay." Rel traced the inner lining on her father's cloak.

Rafe sighed then resumed rubbing Rel's arm.

"Aren't going to ask what's wrong?"

"No," Rafe said.

"Why not?"

"What will the answer do for me, daughter?" He leaned his chin on Rel's head.

"Make you mad."

"What happens when I'm mad?" Rafe gave her a squeeze before pulling away.

"Wolves get hurt," Rel replied.

Rafe shook his head and said, "No, they die."

Rel squeezed his big hand. "You wouldn't do that."

He pulled Rel close, hugging her tightly. He kissed the top of her head then rested his chin on the place he kissed. "The time before I found my way to your mother, Grace, and you, I was rabid."

He rubbed her back as he tightened his embrace. "I am a killer, daughter. I have no qualms with taking a life, especially when it comes to those I love." His grip on Rel eased. "There's so much blood staining my soul."

Rel patted his arm.

Rafe returned the gesture. He got up and kissed the top of her head again. "Refresh yourself and rest." He walked to the door. "Tomorrow your training begins," he said then left.

Rel stared after him wondering what kind of training she'd undergo. Fatigue and hunger cut her musings short. She took her bath and ate the meal left for her and fell into a troubled slumber.

Chapter 16
Father and Daughter

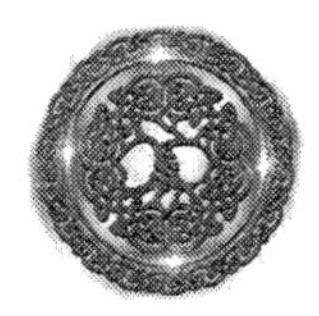

Rel had never seen the Hasking Stone. She pressed her face to the glass like a child, mesmerized by its brilliance. The large pulsating crystal was tucked in a nest of smaller crystals. She'd heard of the Hasking Stone. Learned that it was a divine object. Luna's power spending sixty-two years voluntarily confined to her mother's territory wasn't a torture. The few times she ventured out she got into fights. Not that she minded the fights. Her mother thought it would be good for her to get to know firsthand how the pack worked. It was a must if she hoped to become a proper healer. Rel needed to learn werewolves and their euman side.

The stone was clear like the glass shielding it. Rafe walked her through the different colors and their meanings. They were colors she'd never see because they manifested while she was inside. Since she was in training, the Hasking Stone was clear.

Her experience on Elderton would be defined by several colors. Once she walked into the pack's house, the stone would turn orange. In times when she thrived, the stone would become a nice shade of blue. Yellow meant she was in deep shezia. Red meant shezia was mega deep. She didn't want to think of black, but Rel set her sights on keeping the Hasking Stone purple. Black was not an option. Black meant she was dead, and the pack was cursed. So, no.

After she and Rafe went over the particulars of the stone, he pulled her over to a pair of mats. He sat on one, and she the other. There, they meditated for hours. In between meditation, he asked her questions. Rel's thighs were burning from sitting cross-legged on a hard floor. In less than two days, she would be escorted to Elderton by Ulmer's handpicked guard. Once they docked, Rel would have to survive on her own, and survival wouldn't involve prayers and meditation.

"How is this training?" Rel still flinched at the sound of her disembodied voice. Her mouth moved, but the sound flowed from the ether.

"What did I teach you about the Wilds?" Rafe said, remaining in his meditative pose. Legs crossed. Eyes closed. Hands on his knees.

"Be a wolf cloaked in Bleet's wool."

Rafe nodded, motioning for her to continue.

"My euman self is easily deceived. Trust my instincts. Trust my wolf," Rel chimed. Her lips turned up into a pout. Rel huffed, exasperated by his calm.

"What's that look for?"

"I don't have a wolf," Rel stated plainly.

Rafe's eyes transformed from dark gray to an intense amber. "My wolf comes when I call. Sometimes, he steps in when my euman self needs him."

Rel cocked her head, thoughtful. "My beast lends me her senses, claws, and fangs. She makes me faster. I've never had her just show up."

"Our wolves are not just weapons." He held out his hands which shifted into a claw. His fingers had an extra joint. The knobby protrusions of bone were just as deadly as his claws. They were as hard as stones. Should a werewolf throw a punch without claws, it could, and usually did, shatter the bones of lesser creatures.

Rel touched his fingers, dragging her euman along the slopes of his fingers. "How is a wolf not a weapon?" Rel said absently as she held his hand, rubbing her thumb along the palm. The skin was smooth, like a euman, but the bones and muscle beneath were all were. A perfect marriage of the wolf and the euman.

"My wolf knows when I'm drifting," Rafe said, tapping a knuckle to his head. "I've lived a long a bloody life. As a pup, I thought war was an adventure. That changed quickly once I was immersed in it. In the distance, it's a fantasy where the hero is always brave, and the enemy is always easy to recognize.

Villains do villain things." Rafe rubbed his chest; his knuckles made a hollow sound when they knocked against the bone of his chest. "As new adults, we rush into it. Fighting is exhilarating, but murder isn't. Killing should happen only when necessary. In war, an enemy is a label. The being on the other side of a fight is like me. They live, breath, love, and regret. In war, I kill that father or brother. After the war is when his ghost and others come for me." Rafe reclaimed his hand as he looked past Rel. "I'm sure you've seen me on patrols."

"Yes," Rel said. "Some nights you're different. Your walk is normal." Rel shook her head. "No, you move like a predator. More agile. Graceful, but your eyes are scary."

"I walk the Wilds to keep myself busy. Movement helps. When I'm still, I have time to think. When I think, the memories return. Inside those memories are all the people I've killed. It makes me restless."

"You go on patrol."

"Yes and no." A wistful expression bloomed.

"What do you mean, yes and no?"

"When I go on patrol, my wolf reasons with me."

"So, your wolf talks to you."

"You could say that." Rafe chuckled. "I like to take walks as a euman. The elements feel different. Breezes feel nice on bare skin, but besides the touchy feely bit of nature, I need my wolf to sus out trespassers. It reminds me that life has many parts, and death is the most important. It makes me pause; enjoy the breaths I take. It shows me how to find the lesson in my actions and how to adapt."

Rafe sighed, rubbing his palms across the tops of his thighs. "It reminds me that I am a two natured being. That I'm never alone. It replays my years of wandering when I ran from ghosts. It led me to you." His lopsided grin spread to Rel. "I learned the value of using both parts of myself. The wolf and my euman. Sometime, reason must rest, and your instincts should lead."

"My beast never speaks." Rel shrugged. "It is mute like me."

Rafe shook his head and said, "Your beast may not speak, but it shows itself." He arched his right brow. "It comes when you call, and it comes when you need it, am I right?"

Rel agreed with a short nod.

Rafe held his arms out to the side, palms up, elbows even on each side, mimicking a scale. "My father told me a story. We have two wolves under our skin. One is feral. It likes to bite and runs full speed toward its death." His left arm dipped low as his right arm rose. "We have another that reasons. It is good. Always seeking safety, knowledge, and kinship." Rafe pulls his arms up and down, like the baskets of a scale. "Those two wolves fight for dominance inside us. The fight is constant. They whisper to us. Drive our thoughts. Our actions. But we determine which wolf wins." Rafe stilled, returning his hands to his lap.

"How do you do that if there's so much noise in your head?" Rel's voice spiraled around them.

"You have to be quiet," Rafe said, as he flowed into his meditative posture. "Bring both wolves before you. Sus out their motives. Filter their desires through what you've learned in this life. What's been beneficial for you. What has not. A rule that applies to all living beings, 'actions have consequences.'" He jerked his chin at her. "What marks will your actions leave on others?"

"Like Mother."

Rafe nodded. "Before you act, what do you consider?"

"If Mom would approve or not."

"Why?"

"I want my heart to be like hers." Rel rang her hands. Her disembodied voice crescendo in desperation. "She heals. She makes things better." She smoothed her hands out across her lap. "Our family is a collection of broken spirits. None of us our bound by blood, but her ways...her nature is the balm that keeps us together."

"That's the wolf that thrives inside." Rafe patted his chest. "The dominant wolf is well fed. Its lesser is not."

Rel crawled over to Rafe and plopped down beside him. She lay her head on his shoulder.

"Why do you think the goddess has called us again?" Rafe leaned his head on Rel.

"I don't know."

"Don't be lazy," Rafe admonished her. "Think about what she cherishes. What has the pack done?"

"The pack has no reverence for life." Rel leaned back, using her elbows as props. "Everyone bites and nips at the other," she said, waving a frustrated arm around her head. "I mean, I helped

Draega's pup, but I could tell she wanted no parts of me. Hated me because I could do something she couldn't."

"Draega's ways are my brother's influence. Everyone must prove themselves. Have something to offer to the whole," Rafe said. "It's a terrible thing to find yourself lacking." He huffed. "Wolves adapt. For our pack, most have learned to be the extreme part of their natures. Ulmer's adoptive sons embrace their darkness. They kill to please their dominant him."

Rafe slumped. It looked uncomfortable. "Our pack is doing its best to survive," he said.

"But they're eating each other alive," Rel said.

"Their oppressors are too strong, so they must prey upon each other. The act of dominance, no matter how small or underhanded, satisfies something in the wolf. Dominance or safety. Our wolves want both. Too much of one warps us."

"I don't see how any of this is going to prepare me for the House of Testing," Rel groused.

"This has everything to do with the House of Testing."

"How?" Rel threw up exasperated hands. "Aren't tests all about the fight?" The pack tested Rel whenever she walked among them. Her oddness made her something to be tested. Like pups introduced to new creatures or the few magical devices allowed in the pack. They were curious. Curiosity nips and scratches at the unfamiliar. Rel had the marks to prove it.

Rafe knocked on his head. "The house is going to test your mind." He slapped his palm against his chest. "It's about this, too."

Rafe took Rel's hands in his. "From the moment you walk into that house, your purpose is to find the Hasking Stone inside."

Rel's brows arched, but she did not respond.

"The house is going to do everything it can to make you forget why you're there."

"How am I supposed to find the Hasking Stone if the house is hiding it?" Rel replied.

"Each trial you complete will lead you closer to the Hasking Stone. Any trial you fail will make the next challenge harder. The harder the trial, the easier it is for you to get caught up in the event and fail to learn the lesson."

"So, the house is trying to teach me something," Rel huffed.

"The trails are the goddess's version of the Dominance Fights."

"So, she aims to kill us," Rel said.

"The goddess wants her creations to thrive. Remember what my brother said about Dominance Fights. They reveal the inner nature of the wolf. In a fight to the death, the mind must be quick, adaptable, and always working out the end game. The goddess seeks to expose our inner nature. It's not to torture us but to reset us. Make us aware of her divine will. Not to mention, this world is hers, and we are the caretakers. If we mess up our world, what do you think would happen?"

"It all sounds hard," Rel said, a sense of dread rising.

"You can do this," Rafe encouraged. "You're the only one who can."

"How can I? I don't have time to train like the others."

Rafe grabbed her chin between his thumb and index finger. "There are six things you need to keep in mind when you're in the thick of it. They are: What is the thing you hate? It will haunt you in the house. What is it you dread? The house will deliver. What is your greatest desire? The house will put it before you. It will dangle the answers to mysteries that remain unsolved. What do you fear? It will test your willingness to do what it takes to win. For the remainder of our time together, we will go through them. I don't require an answer. All of this will shape your trials."

Rel slumped on her mat, burying her hands in her hair. "This is crazy."

Rafe pulled back his tunic, revealing a shimmering gold goddess tree. It wasn't the whole tree, just a quarter of it. He tapped his index finger over the symbol. "You won't be alone in there. If you need me, you call me. You can do this three times. If I see you're in jeopardy, I can reach out to you, but I only get one chance."

Rafe gripped Rel's shoulders gently, touching his head to her nose. "You'll know everything I know about surviving the trials by sunset. You'll make it," Rafe said. "I promise."

He kissed her forehead and said, "If you feel the desire to contact me, your mother, or Grace, in the camp there is a statue of a bird. Write your letter. Once you finish writing, that statue will become its true self. It will deliver it to us."

Rafe gave her a final pat on the hand before diving into their lessons again. He was faithful to his promise and drilled Rel on the ins and outs of the challenges. By sunrise on the following day, Rel knew the challenge questions by heart. She rolled them over and over in her head as Rafe escorted her to meet Ulmer's guard who waited at the mouth of the maze. A company of six soldiers. Rel only knew one, their general, Ho'yee.

None of the wolves offered a name nor did they bother. A large russet werewolf bowed before her. Rel's legs refused to move. Once she hopped onto the russet wolf's back, he would take her to the port. There, the company of six males and Rel would be transfered to a small boat that delivered them to Elderton.

Ho'yee lifted a hand to shove her forward.

"If you want to lose that arm, touch her," Rafe growled.

Ho'yee lowered his hand, standing aside as Rafe walked up.

"Sihasin." He bent, touching his forehead to hers. "It's your time to stand for your family. Farah needs you." He gripped her shoulders and squeezed then backed away.

Rel mounted the russet werewolf, who the others called Zee. Her hands gripping the tuft of fur at the back of his neck. Zee rose to his feet.

Chapter 17
On the Banks of Elderton

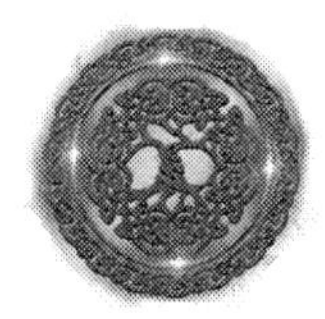

It didn't take long for Rel's escort to travel from the Alpha's Fist to the closest port. The brunt of their journey was spent navigating the Caspeson sea in a midsized sailboat. As they closed in on the island, Ho'yee ordered the sails lowered, and they rowed for the rest of the way.

Wolves weren't keen on large bodies of water. Not that they couldn't swim, but they preferred not to. Bleet drawn carts or on the legs of their beasts were the favored methods of travel. Rel didn't mind the ocean. Rhythmic strokes and splashing oars to water allowed Rel to sink into oblivion. There was no need to think as four wolves worked the oars. Ho'yee sat on the bench beside her. For once, he ignored her.

She faced away from the bow. Elderton loomed. Its presence was palatable, like a hand to her back, much like the warmth of Ho'yee's steady breathing. The warmth of his breath was a brief reprieve from the crisp night air.

Rel tucked her cloak tighter, though it did little against the chill. Unlike the wolves sharing the boat with her, she lacked their pelts. She cut her eyes at the russet wolf facing her. Its gleaming white battle helm carved from Bharg bone added to its menace. Strapped across its chest was a breastplate fashioned from black wood. Swirling glyphs filled with silver and blue dye decorated the edges. The russet wolf sat on its haunches; gaze fixed on the shoreline.

Though every sentient being knew of Elderton, only champions had ever passed through its gates. Rel found it hard to believe that an entire island full of houses designated for every being in her world existed. Words were only true once hands touched, eyes saw, noses smelled, and tongues tasted. It was real.

It was real.

This was happening.

She would soon enter its gates and find the pack's house. Rel pulled her knees close, wrapping her arms around them and laying her forehead on the tops. She missed her mother. Her jaws tightened, teeth agitating her gums, as she worked through the outrage. The disappointment in herself. Her gentle mother was in the hands of Ulmer. If she didn't complete the trials, her mother would die.

Rel swallowed, doing her best to push away the dark thoughts growing like weeds in her psyche. Mother Farah had a saying about it. Darkness rotted away hope. Absence of hope heightened death's appeal. The hopeless raced into the arms of death. Once those arms embraced you, there was no coming back.

Rel canted her head to rub her cheek against the soft fur of her coat. Hints of her mother's scent reviving with every stroke, soothing her as she grasped onto her mother's words. All her life, her mother tempered Rel's darkness with kindness. A healer and the Mvunaji. Her mouth slanted at the bitterness of it. The werewolves of Blacktooth reminded her at every chance through blood, challenges, and whispers of what she was, a living breathing curse.

Rel stiffened when the boat bumped against the shore. She felt Ho'yee's stare. The russet wolf remained seated, though he shifted his weight from paw to paw. Their boat rocked, as behind her, wolves leapt from it to slosh through water. Rel grabbed onto the bench as the small craft jerked forward, then coasted in a wide arc. More wolves leapt from the boat, which rocked violently. To avoid being thrown out, Rel gripped the wood with her claws.

The rocking eased as the little boat emptied. One by one, three of the five wolves in their company were on shore.

Rel's gaze drifted to along the shoreline, noting the tall brass gate surrounding Elderton. There was a dock in the distance.

She craned her neck, wondering if that was the front of the island. It would have been easier if they used it.

"Get out," Ho'yee said before he leapt from the boat.

Rel threw her hands up in a fruitless effort to save herself from being doused. Though the boat was flush with the shoreline, Ho'yee chose to splash in the Bijou. The boat rocked like before, but it wasn't as bad. She looked over at the trio tying complex knots that would keep the boat from drifting away.

"Out!" Ho'yee called from the shore.

Her lip curled as she did as he asked. She fell in line with the company of Fangs gathered on the shore. Ho'yee inspected their form by habit, taking the position closest to the shoreline. This time, Rel wasn't carried on the back of a werewolf, but on her own two feet. Ho'yee had her travel at the heart of the company of six. Being stuck in the middle forced her to keep pace with them. Her stride, militant. They gave the gate a wide berth, but as they jogged, Rel's head turned. The gleam of it catching her eye. She couldn't help but wonder what was on the other side. Rows of houses. Each with their own marker.

By the time their troupe stopped, they stood between the pier and the gate. Rel peeled away from the group, the sheer size of the gate drawing her to it. Brass bars spanned to a great height. From her vantage point, it looked like the top of the gates touched the sky. A small part of her wished she could fly so she could marvel at the intricate curves at the top.

She backed up, cupping a hand over her brow as she continued her inspection. Tendrils of silver light coiled through the gate's bars. It spiced the air with its strange scent. It wasn't like any magic she'd ever come across. There was no malevolence. It didn't spit at her nor was it odious. It was clean. As pure and as a clear as Sprig. There was a rhythm to it. A wispy tinkling of tiny bells. She was tempted to lean closer for a better listen but decided against it. Instead, she watched from her place, the long quiet road on the other side of the gate's intricate design. The gaps between them were wide enough for her to see the goddess mark etched along a stone wall inside. Sharp sloping roof tops broke through the shadows like teeth.

She flexed her nostrils out of habit, ears twisting in search of signs of life. Rocks crunched on the other side. There was something trailing them. Watching. Rel took a cautious step back. She swallowed, surprised she didn't crash into Ho'yee or one of his minions. Rel turned around.

Ho'yee's company maintained a healthy distance. All of them fixated on the gleaming brass gate.

"Live," Ho'yee barked at her before giving the command for his Fangs to withdraw. Six wolves did an about face. Ho'yee melted into a pale gray wolf. He yipped then dashed off toward the boat. The others followed.

Alone standing before an immense gate infused with the magic of the goddess, Rel took a deep cleansing breath and walked forward. With every step, she wondered how she was going to get into Elderton, as she looked for a latch of some kind and found none. She scanned the center of the gate. Rel was able to recognize it as such from the Mother Tree set at the top center. Indolent bursts of golden light flickered between the stylized leaves. She took another step, another gulp of air, and grabbed the bars. She pushed, and the gate swung open, sending her stumbling across the threshold. She was amazed she managed not to fall on her face. Rel looked over her shoulder as the gate slammed shut behind her, sealing her in absolute darkness.

Chapter 18
Luna's Message

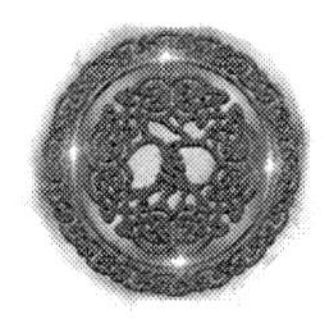

Rel didn't move as a wave of vertigo hit her. She felt weightless. Her toes flexed, finding neither dirt nor stone underfoot. Had she crossed over into the Deadlands?

A tiny luminous speck, barely visible, formed in the void. Rel was tempted to run toward it. Her need to see was strong, but wisdom kept her in place. She was on the island of Elderton. Though her mentor said nothing of testing outside of their assigned house, the strangeness of her surroundings made her wary.

The small light drifted closer, thinning into a long, shimmering silver line. Closer and closer the light came. A dazzling cloud of silver and blue burst forth, mirroring the color of the moons. Light particles spiraled into a funnel then broke apart, revealing a lupine form very much like a werewolf but not quite. Its limbs were leaner. Longer. The ears were sharper at the tips. Its tail did not feather along the bone with long fur like a werewolf. The fur was short. Its glowing eyes were not the same color. The left was silver, while the right was blue. Both were iridescent. The creature's trot had a predatory grace, and it did not falter until it stopped just out of reach, tantalizingly close.

Rel fell to her knees the moment she realized the creature in front of her was the goddess Luna. She'd heard of the goddess. Prayed to her from time to time. She never once thought the goddess heard her or cared. Luna was a goddess of werewolves, of which Rel was not. Why would her soul's words find her ears?

She fell prostrate before the goddess, hoping for forgiveness. Hands curling in the open air, wishing for dirt or leaves to twist. The sound of something breaking would make her feel better.

Disembodied laughter floated around her. It was everything she imagined a god's voice to be. Light. Melodious like the hollow glass chimes, Mother Farah hung near the windows of their little cottage. The tautness of Rel's body waned. She lifted her head in time to see the goddess shift from her lupine form into a silver-white pulsating fissure which melted into a euman. Silver-white locs floated around her head. Wisps of it bobbing around her golden-brown face as if caught in their own wind current. The goddess donned a sleeveless dress which draped her curves flaring out from the hips. The fabric pooled around her. It shimmered like it was full of stars.

Luna clasped her hands, pressing them against her chin.

"Forgive my disrespect, goddess."

Disembodied laughter flickered around Rel like Dragon's Breath pollen. Blue and silver starbursts drifted like dying stars to the ground.

"Wolves are nothing if not disrespectful," the goddess replied.

Rel's heart seized.

"Do not fret, daughter. You are not like most wolves."

Rel gazed into the silver-blue gaze of her goddess.

"My wolves have not learned their lesson," the goddess said, as she paced a short line before Rel.

Rel's brows arched at the goddess's words.

"What lesson?" Rel's voice ascended into the darkness then vanished like a vapor.

"What is an alpha, daughter?"

"A dick," Rel muttered.

Peels of disembodied laughter filled the vast space. Its touch was light on her skin. Like bubbles, they burst, emitting the scent of moon flowers.

Rel pressed her lips together. Doing her best not to join the goddess in her delight. A goddess always came bearing warnings. At least, that was what many of the wolves in the pack said.

"You speak a truth that is undeniable, but for the task ahead, its meaning is crucial."

Rel sobered as she observed the goddess before her. A sense of kinship bloomed in her chest. The goddess's form was neither wolf, were, nor euman. Rel narrowed her eyes, summoning her beast. Darkness remained, though Rel expected to see an array of the strange fissures. Her nose flexed. There was no decay, only the clean, crisp odor of magic she had scented at the gate.

"Again, daughter, what is an alpha?"

Rel searched for words that shaped what she knew an alpha to be. Her lips parted, and the charm the alpha gave her glowed. "An alpha is cruel. He leads with sharp teeth and claws. It is not beneath him to kill his own for the sake of submission. An alpha values strength and obedience. The alpha is predator, and the pack is prey."

Luna's beautiful face remained impassive. She tapped the space over her heart. "Is that what you believe, daughter?"

Rel's brows furrowed as she slowly shook her head while an answer took root. "I know of no other way for an alpha to be," she said.

"If it were up to you, what is an alpha?" Luna asked.

"An alpha should look after a pack like a herder cares for livestock. A herder protects his livestock. He chooses what is best for the herd to thrive."

Rel twisted one of her locks around her finger as she considered what she said. "An alpha shouldn't terrorize his pack."

Luna seemed satisfied with Rel's answer and asked another. "What is the pack to the alpha?"

The question surprised Rel. To the pack, the alpha was alpha. His commands were law. It had always been that way.

"The pack is a herd. Strays are only as valuable as what they provide the pack." Rel blinked at the harshness of her own words.

"Daughter, consider my question as you enter the House of Testing." Luna bowed her head. The hand over her heart closed into a fist.

Luna reached for Rel. Her hand freezing barely an inch away from her face before she drew it away.

"It's up to you to define what the pack is and what it needs." Luna backed away from Rel, her steps creating waves of light which flowed out from the soles of her feet across the inky black surface she stood upon.

"Victory will be found in your greatest desire and under the bitterness of truth. What you accept will bring either a curse or free the pack."

With that, Luna turned around and walked away. With each distancing step, the surrounding light intensified. The euman body of the goddess spiraled into her four-legged form, a spectral wolf of silver and blue light. The wolf swung its head in Rel's direction. There was a sadness in Luna's eyes when they settled on Rel.

"I hope you are not broken by what you see." Luna's words filled her mind. A divine resonance, like soft thunder and ice. The spectral wolf blinked, then dashed off into the darkness. A silver mist spread out like a path before it. At the end, a bright starburst formed in the shape of a half moon. The spectral wolf's run did not falter, even as the starburst stretched wide and swallowed it whole.

Rel had to close their eyes due to the brilliance of the starburst. The light was blinding, and no amount of hand-covering could dull its radiance. Rel pressed her hands over her face and bowed her head until the spots in her sight faded. When she finally opened her eyes, she stood at the edge of a campsite.

Chapter 19
Grace

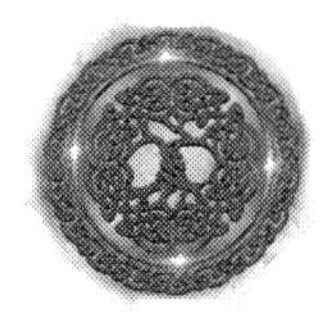

Grace's gift was her diminutive size. As a dougan, the pack considered her harmless, which allowed her to move freely among them. Sure, there was the occasional growl or threat of being eaten. Their threats were empty. A wolf preferred a challenge. It helped her carry out her true master's wishes while aiding her Adí.

Her Adí tasked her with the honor of guarding their matriarch.

She banked left, webbed feet tight against her body with wings spread wide, allowing the rising air to carry her. She glided effortlessly above the clouds. With the Eldritch Trials in full swing, the alpha's paranoia peeked. Most of the alpha's Mgwans were dispatched to keep watch over the Commons. The few that remained were tucked within the canopy below, but that didn't bother her.

Mgwans were harbingers of magic. The birds themselves were not magical. Any magic they carried was poured into them by a handler. Grace's wings beat against the air, the tips riding the current as she collected sparks of wild magic drifting on the wind. Another beat of her wings, and she wrapped magic around her body. Doing so concealed her scent, making her invisible to both Mgwans and the Alpha's Fangs.

Grace needed to find Mother Farah for her Adí. She banked right, letting the wind carry her into a funnel of warm air above the alpha's compound. It pulled her into a wide circle over the back half of the alpha's buildings.

In her duck form, her magic was hidden within the hollows of her bones. Once she shifted, the Mgwans and any nearby alchemists would detect her presence. She had to get inside before she shed her avian form. If she was lucky, she would shift inside the lower levels. Specifically, the dungeons. They were spelled to keep the alpha's secrets hidden from those using the skyways over their land. Since war between citizens of Eldritch were forbidden, what he kept hidden there would cause many to break that law.

Grace flapped her wings, adding more speed to her flight while gliding higher. She needed an opening.

Grace weaved and dove deeper, slipping between the branches, sinking beneath the canopy. A little silver charm shaped like a crescent moon darkened. As it did, so did Grace's body. She glided past the Mgwans, who after a cursory glance, returned to their avian preening. Her shadowed form was an errant breeze. A trembling of leaves and nothing more.

As she drew closer to the Alpha's compound, she searched for open windows, sunrooms with a sliding pane. After a few passes, she spotted the Arena. Its dome was open. She swooped in, keeping close to the walls, mindful of the sonar stones along the viewing room.

The pungent aroma of urine, feces, and blood spiced the air as she neared the fighter's ring. Swirling grooves from a rake decorated the ground. The arena floor had been recently tilled. Prominent deep red marks littered the pale brown dirt. Weapons filled the racks on the north and south end of the ring. The rest was bare open space, allotting fighters plenty of room to murder one another for the alpha's entertainment.

Grace flew toward the south door, shifting into her euman form as she descended. She pulled from the collection of blood embedded in the tilled soil, feeding it into the magic fueling her shift. If she was going to fulfill her Adí's wishes, she had to get stronger.

Grace possessed a strength common among shifters, but she needed more than her gender could offer. She checked the access door at the end of the corral. A thick polished brown door separated her from the hall which fed into the staging area where armor and weapons were kept for training. A werewolf participating in a Dominance Fight was required to bring their own arms. Most owned their own body armor. Grace checked the area above and across from her for sonar stones. Satisfied that there were none present, she surrendered to the shift.

A spasm racked her body as she landed between the wall separating the contenders from the crowd. Her teeth clicked together, as blades of pain sliced through her bones as they stretched. Fine bones pushed against her skin, arching her back, pulling her mouth open in a scream that did not come. Her throat constricted around the shifting bones. A lump rose at its center, sending Grace into a violent coughing fit.

She rolled onto her side, her body folding as her pubic bone fractured. Her arms felt like slabs of stone, but she managed to lift them in time to silence a rising scream. Locking her jaws against a wave of convulsions, she bore the pain as her pelvis narrowed, and her chest broadened. Tendons and muscles blazed as they lengthened to realign with the change to her body. Time was crucial to her mission, but agony didn't care. It held her in its teeth, pinning her to the ground until the inner workings of her shift ended.

Grace lay still, panting, fingers digging into the tilled dirt as the burning radiating along the joints ebbed to a point where she felt capable of movement. She rolled onto her back and forced herself to sit upright.

It hurt to turn her head.

Jiiq, it hurt to blink.

For a moment, she stared at the stone slab that was the barrier wall. The coolness of the mirror behind her tempted her to turn, but she needed a few more seconds. She pulled her knees tightly against her body. Her muscles responded to the stretch. She hugged her legs, drawing her shoulders forward, and rolled them. This new body liked movement.

Grace leaned back, examining her new legs. They were longer and bulkier. A trail of dark gray hairs flowed from her thighs, ending above her ankles. The bracelet Mother Farah gave her sparkled in the waning sunlight.

Grace ran her hands across her chest. Gone were her tiny teacup sized breasts. They had been replaced by two solid lumps of hard muscle. She applied her fingernails to her exploration, enjoying the sensation when they grazed the nipples. There was hair on her chest. Her fingers burrowed into it and pulled. The hair was coarse. She looked down, pressing her chin to her neck to get a better view of its coloring. Purple-brown hairs coiled around Grace's fingers. She grinned.

She liked her new body, deciding she needed to explore it more. She stood up, looking over her shoulder she examined her back. Impressed by its sloping planes which tapered down to a perfectly plump plu, which she flexed. Grinning like an idiot, she took a deep breath, and turned around. Mouth agape, Grace feasted on the taller male version of herself. Metal gray eyes peered back at her. Her dark green heart shaped face was much broader. She tilted it up, running a hand along an angular jawline covered in short coarse hair.

This new body was long and well-muscled. Hair grew in places not normal to her old body. Grace ran her hands down her chest, enjoying the planes of newly formed muscles. Her feminine body had muscles, but they weren't as rigid. Where her feminine waist dipped in, and her hips flared, this masculine form was a sleek line, which tapered down to lean hips.

Grace gaped at the change between her legs. She spread them and wiggled her hips, giggling at the penis bouncing between them. She couldn't wait to figure out how that worked. For the time being, it would come in handy for the challenge ahead. The alpha only allowed male guards the run of the dungeons.

Grace gave herself a final once over. Her body qualified her as guard material. Now, all she had to do was get her hands on a uniform. Once she had one of those, she could figure out the rest. Mother Farah was home. Family. No matter where she was in Eldritch, Grace could find her.

She had to get going. If she was going to keep watch over Mother Farah, she needed to start procuring all the necessary items that would help her do so. First, she needed to blend in among the wehrs.

Closing her eyes, she recited the prayer Mother Farah taught her. Her skin tingled with the first word spoken.

"May the Eyes of Luna light my path, Granting me the gift of your silver eye.Obscure my natural body from the wolves.Let their eyes see my euman skin as pack. Should this body be required to fight, Gift me claws and fangs to stand my ground.Blessed Luna, I thank thee for your favor."

With the rising of her head, the tingling around her body ceased. Perfect white teeth flashed in the mirror from a handsome brown face. Her euman body was the same brown as her face. Grace's metal-gray eyes remained the same. Long black ropes of hair cascaded down her back. She winked at her image, bent to liberate the satchel her Adi gave her, then set off to find her matriarch.

Chapter 20
Camping with Champions

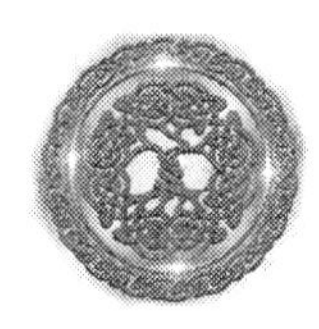

Soft golden light framed the cluster of manicured shrubs lining the trail as she walked. It reminded her of the Alpha's Fist with its twisted beauty. Beautiful poison adorned the maze. Gleaming red Lancing fruit hung at several points along the maze. It was easily mistaken for a Lon fruit. Both fruit were red but the Lancing to touch. If one was unlucky enough to peel away the skin, they would see the black flesh inside. It was sticky and smelled sweet. It killed within minutes of being handled.

Rel doubted the goddess meant her harm, but she kept her arms tight against her body as she continued along the path. It was straightforward. Above the shrubs and wild trees, wood poles protruded. The closer she got, the more she realized that the bright white swaths of cloth were tied around the wooden stakes. Tents! Calm blues and muted yellows became visible as she continued down the trail. Something hissed, spinning her around as she searched frantically for the source. Rel reasoned that there had to be a Naga nearby or something like it. Nagas were serpent shifters. She wasn't a fan of serpents. The Naga were citizens of Elderton. She had nothing against them. She had never met one, but considering the type of shifter they were, Rel thought it best to avoid them all together.

As she neared camp, a new amalgam of noises surfaced. Roars, caws, and a thing with a predatory laugh congealed in a haunting melody. One that made her skin crawl and her beast uneasy. Rel looked around for a place to sit. A place that hid her from the others. An area apart from the camp that would allow her to come to grips with all the sounds and smells.

She found a spot along the gate between a cluster of trees. There was enough to provide coverage. She took a cursory look up at the sky. There were no stars, yet there was enough light for her to get around. It was like being caught when the sun lingered on the horizon. Dark, but not absolute. She inspected the trees sheltering her. Could she climb one, and if she did, would she find branches, serpents, or spindles? Spindles were worse than serpens with their ten long multi-jointed legs. They moved like swinging ropes. Small, round bodies amid all those legs made her skin crawl.

Focusing on the surrounding trees, Rel pressed her foot against the trunks and pushed. Out of the three she sheltered under, the one closest to the gate did not bend. She searched for a low branch.

"Need some help?"

Rel spun into a fighter's stance. A red-haired euman watched Rel with interest. Amber eyes held the glow of the surrounding firelight. Light spread its fingers into the clearing where Rel stood. It rose, framing the euman who joined her, revealing an array of stripes. The glow seemed to wet her hair, giving the ends the quality of blood.

"No...no...um...no I don't need any help," Rel replied.

Instantly, annoyance appeared on the red-haired female's face. "What's up with you?" She leaned away from Rel, pointing at her mouth. "How did you do that?"

"What?" Rel looked around, wondering what she missed.

The red-haired human pointed at Rel's mouth.

Rel pointed at herself. Finger pressed against her lips.

"You're talking, but your mouth's not moving."

Rel pointed at the Favor Stone around her neck. "Magic. Without it, I can't speak at all."

The red-haired euman inched closer with a hand poised to touch. She stopped short of crossing into Rel's personal space.

"What are you?" Rel asked. The euman stared at the Favor Stone, blinked, then looked up at Rel.

"I'm a chimera," red hair said. "How about you?" She gestured toward Rel. "Are you some kind of feline?"

"No," Rel said.

"So, you're a werewolf," the red-haired human said.

"I'm only half," Rel said it like it was a confession.

"I guess that's why those wolves that brought you were actin' weird."

"Those were my guard," Rel replied.

"Are you some kind of royalty?" The red-haired euman grinned. "I've already a met princess."

Rel shook her head vigorously. "I'm not royalty of any kind." She shrugged. "I guess you could say I'm less than a peasant."

"Werewolves don't like hybrids?"

"Werewolves barely like werewolves," Rel mumbled under her breath.

"I guess we're in a similar situation," the red-haired euman said. She stepped forward, thrusting her hand out. "I'm Denai."

Their hands met with a clap. Rel shook Denai's hand. "I'm Rel," she said, as she assessed Denai. "So, your people treat you like a stray?"

Denai laughed at that. "You could say that. I was raised among the leanu. You would think they could show a sista' some affection. At least treat me like a cousin, but nooooo." Denai rolled her eyes, spun in a quick circle, and threw exasperated arms in the air. "I'm constantly having to hand lyna's their plu's 'cause they let their feelings get the best of them."

Denai pressed her hands in her chest as she looked sideways at Rel. "When they get in they feelings, I get in mine. An emotional lyna and a chimera together equals brawl."

They both laughed from their guts.

It feels good to let loose, Rel thought.

Rel raised her hand, saluting Denai. "Tell me about it," she said. "All I have to do is occupy a space and trouble comes for me."

"Hmph," Denai said, looking off toward the camp. "Sista," Denai giggled. "

Rel liked Denai's ready endearments. It felt weird, but it was a good weird. She felt accepted. Her oddness didn't matter. Not once did Denai ask about her skin or anything else.

Denai looked off toward the distant line of homes. There were rows of them. A field of houses as far as the eye could see formed an arc around the camp.

"I have to go," Denai said, her focus on the houses.

"Your challenge?"

Denai nodded. "This is it for me as far as dawdling." She took a deep breath and blew it out through pursed lips. The air creating a soft whistle. Denai jogged toward the trail and stopped. She looked over her shoulder at Rel.

"It was nice meeting you," Denai said. "Please make sure you grab a tent. There's food and other provisions inside. You can't get any of that hanging out here in the shadows."

"I will," Rel promised.

"Besides, every species in the camp is focused on the upcoming trial. Very few will acknowledge you, much less cause trouble."

Rel giggled. "Trouble's why we're all here."

"Right," Denai said. "It was nice meeting your hybrid, Rel."

Rel could tell she meant it.

Denai waved before trotting down a trail that led into the outer row of houses. Rel watched her until she disappeared into the sea of homes.

She decided to take Denai's advice and headed into the campgrounds.

Rel pulled back the tent flap and ducked in. Inside was cozy. There was a cot, a small end table with a covered basket on top. Rel could tell from the smell that it was food. A sleeve of water was propped against the table. Rel sat down on the cot and made short work of the food. She couldn't eat anything the night before she traveled with the Fangs. With the boat ride, meeting a goddess and a chimera, she was beat.

She flopped onto the cot, pulling her legs up. She looked around the room, noting a desk with fresh paper and pen on top. She lay on the cot, searching for the station Rafe told her about. So many sounds filtered in from the outside. Her ears twitched, swiveling toward strange laughter. It was deep, rumbling like thunder. Another voice was sharp, high-pitched. The gender of the owner was hard to discern. So much noise should have made it impossible for her to feel lonely, but she did.

While she lay on a cot on an island far away from home, her mother suffered in a cell under the alpha's care. Rel was certain Ho'yee, and his company had crossed out of the Bijou into the Caspeson sea. It should take them half a day to get back. Another five or six hours after docking for them to reach the Alpha's Fist. Ho'yee would run to Ulmer and report like a good little Fang. If she wrote a letter now, would the Umital bird get it to her mother without any problems?

Rel scooted the chair closer to the desk, smoothed out the paper, and rolled the pen under her fingertip. What could she write? She dragged her finger across the smooth surface of the page.

Rafe told her that death was rare during the trials, but what if she was the first in the pack to die? During one of their sessions, he rattled off the history of the pack's winners and losers. There were more winners than losers.

The reality of what lay ahead for her was oppressive. Fear placed the pen in her hand, and guilt added words to paper.

Mother,

~~*I'm sorry my temper got the best of me. You always said it would be my undoing.*~~

Sorry, Mother.

Sorry.

It is the only word I have, though I know it holds neither weight nor meaning, considering what I've done. You must understand that being complacent wears on me. I'm not built for it, though it works well within the Pack~~, but we are not Pack. No~~.

I am not Pack.

Why is it so hard to write this letter? It should pour from the depths of my soul, unless I don't have one of those, either. Maybe the Pack is right. I am an abomination. Not just in my look but in my character.

I am not like you. Kind. Wise. Merciful. My rage is constant. It burns hotter in my helplessness. My inability to keep you out of the Alpha's clutches. It is my fault that he has you.

By Luna, I wish I held power, if only for the sake of protecting you. If I were a full werewolf, I would challenge Ulmer. Show the Pack he is no champion but a cruel rabid beast. I would pull his teeth, every one of them if I must.

A dog without its fangs is not a threat. Ulmer is not a true threat. It is the knives he surrounds himself with. His mad dogs and spying birds.

I will survive the House of Testing. I will make it out. Not for the Pack but for you.

I need you to survive.

Be safe. Grace is coming. I gave her something for you. I hope you both can use it. Run away. I hope the Lyew give you refuge. If they do not, there are always the Longtooth.

No matter where you end up, I will find you. Until then, wish me luck. Plead with Luna on my behalf. The goddess hears the prayers of the pure, which I am not.

Always with love,

Your daughter, Rel

It took five tries to finish the message to her mother. When she put the pen down, she heard flapping wings. She turned around. A statue of the Umital bird sat inside the tent beside the flap. Unsure of how it worked, Rel lowered the sealed letter in front of the statue's beak. It opened wide enough for her to slip it inside. Its beak closed on the letter. Blue-white starbursts shimmered, consuming it. Its light intensified as it dissipated. In less than a minute, the status was gone.

Rel stood in front of the entrance for a while, eyes locked on the spot where the status once stood. She hoped her mother and Grace could use the strange orbs. At least having them would give them an option.

Yawning, Rel returned to the cot and lay down. In the morning, she would begin the trek to locate the pack house.

Chapter 21
House of Testing

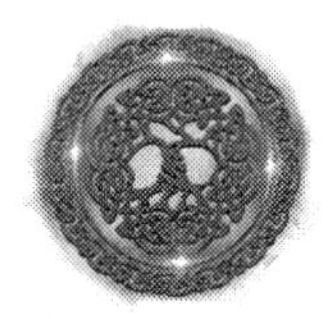

The goddess's message made no sense as Rel trudged across the barren streets of Elderton. Rows of houses loomed, curling, and bending along the many roads. No house was the same. Quaint cottages painted in bright colors, some dull. There were many colors she'd never seen before. Houses in Blacktooth territory were made from the lumber extracted from the forest. Several houses she passed were made from stone like the Arms of Luna but white. There were some carved out of materials that shimmered as if composed of precious jewels. Each of the strange structures tempted Rel to pause her journey long enough to trot up steps or down a short path so she could touch them. She knew if she did, it wouldn't stop with a touch. Her beast would want to learn the smells. Curiosity would call to her and lead her to circle the buildings, look in windows, and examine the exterior. All those things would rob her of time. Finding their house and starting the trials was crucial. The longer it took her to enter the house placed her mother at risk.

Rel curled her hand, flexing it as if it were stiff. The mark didn't burn. It didn't hurt at all. It reminded her of what was at stake. Mother Farah was suffering.

Sure, she sent Grace to look after her, but what would happen to Grace should she get caught by the alpha's Fangs? Would they kill her?

Rel shook away her thoughts, choosing to focus on the rhythm of her steps as she examined the symbols on the doors of the houses. A single-story house made of dark brown wood. It looks as if it survived a fire. Her nose instinctively tested the air for the signs of a fire. Her face twisting in disappointment at the crisp scent of magic.

She stopped at the base of stone steps leading up to a porch in proportion to the house. It was basic, small, with no outer furnishings. It reminded her of a lodge merchants used while on pack land. It was modest. Big enough to hold two bedrooms and a bath. She wondered if it had a kitchen.

Rel trotted up the steps to stand before a reddish-brown door. A gold wolf's head rested in the center of a crescent moon. She traced the gleam of moonlight, relishing the coolness of it. Blacktooth land was lush. Fertile ground for crops and herds, but the pack should be like the land. Thriving, but they weren't. Her hand dropped to the door's nob, which was the same gold as the pack's crest. She stroked the polished surface, unwilling to turn the knob. Once she turned the nob and stepped inside the house, the trials would begin.

Her hand fell to her side as her life flashed before her mind's eye. Rel had never contemplated death, yet on the other side of the door, it could be waiting for her. Why risk it? Her hand brushed against the alpha's morbid reminder. Mother Farah was alive, at least she hoped, back on pack land, but would she remain that way? Rel pressed her knuckles against the smooth wood, letting her weight rest against it. The place looked worn, but the door was solid.

Should she risk her life? Rel thought as she looked over her shoulder to see another creature hurry past her house. It looked eumen like her, but its skin was a deep shade of green. Its hair streamed behind it like a tangle of vines. Its gender was difficult to discern, not because of distance but because its body did not possess the curves and angles familiar to her. The green being darted up the steps of a house four buildings away. They entered without hesitation.

Rel had no love for the pack. The wolves were cruel. Mean. Desperate.

Rel straightened her eyes again on the doorknob. Most of her life she spent fighting. Her beast enjoyed it but her eumen side did not. Would the Testing truly make a different with the pack upon her return? Would any of them care? She saved them from Songga, yet earned their scorn. She stepped back, rubbing her stomach along the way.

Was it worth it?

The question conjured the words of the pup she saved.

"Are you gonna take my soul?" Her nose flexed in remembrance of his terror. Mvunaji. It's what the pup called her. A reaper.

"I'm not here for your soul. I'm here to make you better." Is what she told the pup. If she lingered in her indecision, the brand proved true. To willfully allow the curse was the same as reaping their souls. The pack would die. Not physically, though some would. Their souls would fade away. The spark in them would fade. In time, she feared they would all lie down and let themselves die. Worst of all, her mother would be ashamed and disappointed.

Rel surged forward, grabbed the knob, and turned. She pushed open the door. The idea of breaking her mother's heart sent her across the threshold into the house. The door slammed shut behind her.

A speck of color materialized at the tip of the Hasking Stone, rapidly expanding until the clear stone had turned orange. Ulmer grinned.

"Drakgo!" Ulmer turned to his brother, pointing at the Hasking Stone. "That little fatu. She did it! She entered the House of Testing!"

Something flashed across his brother's face. Rafe blinked and whatever was there was gone. Ulmer knew his brother would never share his thoughts or expose any feelings. It was not their way. Besides, he honestly didn't give a jiiq. Things were going his way. That's all that mattered.

If his instincts were right. The little hybrid would do well in the trials, though he had his doubts of her making it to the end. Luna willing, the female would succeed in the trails. She killed Songga, and Songga was his best. In the sixty-two years of her existence within the pack, the female proved herself. She was tough. A fighter. She'd kicked many plu's and she did so without a wolf. From the reports brought to him by his Fangs, she had never fully shifted. Her claws, teeth, and ears were wolf but the rest of her was something else.

"Let's see how she does with the testing." Ulmer went over to his alpha's seat. He settled in, eyes on the Hasking Stone.

"Rel will succeed." Rafe said.

Ulmer didn't bother to look at his brother. He was fond of the female and was no doubt banging the purple elf. Rafe lived with them in some shack on their land. Land he gave them. As long as Rafe stayed out of his fur, Ulmer ignored them though the pack requested he exile them. The healer served a purpose. Her reputation among the multitude of beings outside Blacktooth borders, especially her familiarity with the Lyew were of great value. She was worth her weight in silons. Since her arrival, trade had increased. Her knowledge of several languages and mastery of Eldish aided in the expansion of pack trade.

Ulmer rubbed his hands together, as he considered how he would use the healer's suffering as a teaching point for Rel. He was certain she believed he would kill the healer.

I'm glad you have confidence brother." Ulmer plucked a Bharg meat kabob from a bowl and tore off a chunk of flesh. He leaned into his chair, contemplating the many methods of torture that would make both females sing their pain. He would drink in their sorrow before relenting. Once Rel was broken, he would add her to his harem. Her pups would strengthen his bloodline.

"You speak as if you wish for the pack to be cursed." Rafe snapped.

Ulmer waved his kabob at his brother. "I wish only for the success of the pack." He leaned forward, tearing off another chunk of meat. He chewed. Swallowed then said, "The hybrid will complete the task." Ulmer flashed a venomous grin. "Her mother's life depends on it.

Rafe glowered at him before stomping from the room.

Ulmer laughed, enjoying his brother's ire. His kabob nearly finished; he lay it on the tray his staff left for him. He stared at the door his brother exited through. Rafe was supposed to die after the Eldritch Trials. He had discussed this with Songga. Now, with no assassin, he was forced to come up with a new plan.

Ulmer clasped his hands together as if offering a prayer to the goddess. Resting the tips against his full, smiling lips. He toyed with the idea of forcing the hybrid to execute him as final payment for her mother's life.

Rafe would be too shocked to defend himself if he could from the female he treated as his pup. Ulmer snickered. Delighted in his genius.

He turned his attention to the Hasking Stone. Its color remained unchanged. He rubbed his chest. The tattoo on his chest reminded him of his legacy. The Blacktooth clan saved the pack. His brother completed the trials. It was a shame the female was not of his line. It was more of a shame that she was not a full werewolf.

The pack would suffer the loss of a little honor in her triumph (if she succeeded) but they would remain free. And maybe, after this win, the pack would not be called to the House of Testing for more than seven years. Maybe this time, Luna would give them her full blessing.

Ulmer grabbed the kabob and finished off the Bharg meat. All the while wondering what his pack did to displease the goddess so.

Chapter 22
A Seed of Hope & Rebellion

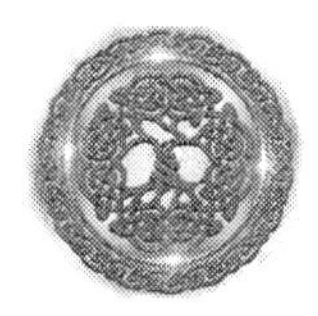

Pups and their mothers were hidden shortly after Rel led away to hide. Every day, their hiding place changed. All within the hidden chambers of the Commons. Out of sight of the alpha's Fangs who patrolled along the edge of their encampment.

Many of the wolves were relieved that the alpha had not taken out his wrath in blood, but none of them were foolish enough to believe that he'd let their discretion slide. To sin against the alpha was a gateway to pain and if he was merciful, a quick death. But every wolf knew Ulmer Blacktooth was not a merciful beast. Mia knew Ulmer's feral side well. The pup she was tasked with attending was a result of it.

Mia immersed a rag in a bowl of medicinal water as her thoughts swirled. The pack's numbers had thinned. The best of them lived in the Alpha's Fist while the weaker pack members existed in the gaps of settlements. Numbers enhanced a wolf's chances of survival. Artisans and merchants were assigned Fangs. Each kept Mgwans on their property to discourage trespassers.

She drew out the rag, wrung it before dabbing it gently along the stitches in the pup's side. Once she finished a few passes, she would apply Candela paste. A snap of wings to her left startled her. She looked up to find a Mgwan perched on a merchant sign. The little skull faced bird preened itself. Lifting its indigo wings, oblivious to his surroundings.

Mia noticed that the presence of Mgwans had increased since the Fangs captured Rel. Word among the Commons was to be mindful of their conversations. The pups were always watched by an adult. Their mouths gave away too many secrets when they were at play. Secrets that could get them killed.

The pup she tended squeezed her wrist.

"Did the Mvunjai return to the Deadlands?" The pup signed.

"Mvunjai?" Mia said aloud. Face contorting in confusion.

The pup nodded.

"What do you mean?"

"The Mvunaji healer who did this." He signed then pointed at the stitches.

Mia withdrew the rag, putting it back in the bowl. She studied the pup. "Why do you think she's in the Deadlands?" Mia wrung out the excess water before applying the final round of medicine.

"She collected the bad wolf's heart." The pup signed frantically. "She weighted it." The pup held up his clawed hand, tilting it like a scale. "After judgment, the gods go home, right?" He signed.

Mia pulled away the rag, weighing the pup's words. No one had ever called Rel a god. She raised the rag to cover her smile as she wondered what Farah would think of the pup's words. She straightened her face. Becoming all business, she asked the pup. "Why do you call Mvunaji a god?"

"Gods give life, and they take it." The pup signed; his eyes full of awe. "The goddess fixed me up. She fought off the bad wolf."

Mia's brow pinched. "Songga." She gestured toward her chest, mimicking the removal of a heart.

The pup shook his head. "No. The one from before." The pup's excited fingers flew. "She made it so me and my mom could get away."

"What is your name?"

"Alder." He signed.

"The Mvunaji is in the Deadlands." Mia replied.

Alder frowned, his fingers were hesitant. "Is she coming back?"

Mia leaned closer to the little wolf. She looked around conspiratorially before whispering. "She went to the Deadlands to beseech the greater goddess Luna on our behalf."

Alder beamed. "She's nice. I think Luna will listen."

Mia's heart warmed at the pup's faith. "I believe she will too." She squeezed his hand, mindful of the claws.

A Mgwan landed beside them, startling the pup. Its beak opened; a tiny pearl of light materialized.

"It is time." The light pulsed in time with the voice. "Your presence is required."

The Mgwan closed it beak and flew away.

"Are you going to the Deadlands now?" Alder's eyes were wide as his fingers asked his question.

"No little wolf. I am not." Mia smiled at the pup before searching for another healer. Finding one, she gave Alder's hand a final squeeze. "Don't fret, little wolf. I'm going to do prepare the way for the Mvunaji's return."

Mia left the pup and headed off to meet her contact. Whether Rel succeeded or failed. The alpha would fall.

Chapter 23
Echo Chamber

There was nothing spectacular about the inside of the house. Rel thought as she lingered in the foyer. It led into a small living area with minimal furnishings. A single cushioned chair, a plain pale brown throw rug adorned the space. The rug lay in front of an unlit fireplace. She cautiously entered the room as she inspected it. To her left was a corridor that seemed to go on forever. Warm light faded as it stretched into absolute darkness. The right side of the wood paneled hall was windowless without adornments. No pictures. No trophies from a hunt. On the left, a row of blue and silver doors, each a different shade stretched into the abyss.

Rel's eyes narrowed at the depth of the corridor. She wondered if it turned left or right, or did it stretch on forever? A few more steps led her into the room's center. She sniffed the air. No signs of another wolf. No food or medicines.

Rel turned her attention back to the room where she stood. The space was conspicuously absent of dust but what held her attention was the fireplace. It was modest, set in the center of the far-left wall. There were two shelves parallel to it. They were set slightly higher than the. Both were bare. She walked over to the fireplace where she crouched to examine the logs. They looked old. Hollowed out and withered by flame. She stooped to touch the log on top of the pile. Dragging her finger along the side, it felt real but when she pulled her finger away, it was clean. No soot.

Rafe warned her that the house would begin testing her the moment she crossed the threshold. She wondered if she was being tested now. Warm air flowed from the throat of the corridor. There was a moistness to it, as if it were the breath of a living beast.

Instinct kept her eyes confined to the living room. Something about the long hall troubled her. She felt if she looked at it, whatever lurked there would come for her. She wasn't ready for a fight yet, wanting to get her bearings.

Rel looked around spotting a figurine on a shelf near the fireplace. It wasn't there before. There had been no personable item inside when she walked into the living room. Rising, she took a few steps away from it, deciding it was best to be wary of it. The figurine was made of wood. Hand craved from the detail of it. Rel pulled the figurine closer as she called her beast to the surface to use its eyes.

Her sight sharpened, allowing her an intrinsic view of its facial features. The figurine was male. A werewolf in its euman skin. The flat face and hawkish nose marked it as pack. He wore armor with the mark of the former alpha on the breastplate. She'd heard werewolves in a time before the curse were claws for hire. They lived to fight and fight they did. There were some wolves in the pack who were from that time. Scars and missing limbs and other parts were their banners. The worst scars were veiled. Hidden behind their eyes, resurrected by careless sounds and sometimes a random phrase. Rel caught glimpses of them when her mother visited their dens. Old warriors preferred living away from the pack. Relying on their feral natures to survive. Unlike the wehrs taking part in the Feral Runs, most of the Elder Fangs sheltered the weak. Wolves taking part in the Runs avoided them. An Elder Fang did not answer to Ulmer, but they did not meddle with his affairs.

Something fell behind her. She spun searching for the source, muscles taut, claws at the ready. A second figurine lay on its side at the lip of the corridor. This one she knew. It was a replica of her mother dressed in armor complete with a sleeve of daggers. Her arms arched above her head poised as if preparing to launch something. Rel was certain it was magic. She looked over at the figurine on the shelf. Werewolves hated magic. They tolerated only what was given to them by the goddess. Those were in the form of sonar stones, the Hasking Stone, and the few artifacts kept by scouts that allowed them to translate the many tongues of beings beyond pack land.

Rel picked up the figurine, turning it over in her hands. Her mind flooded with questions. Mother Farah was a healer. She did not fight. Her tongue was quite sharp when necessary but never had her mother picked up a blade unless it was to prepare a meal or sever thread.

Rel's heart raced at the lethal expression on her mother's face. The brows on the figurine sloped down in a scowl and the lips were a tight line. Even the muscles were drawn for battle. It was so unlike her solemn faced mother.

A soft clicking echoed down the hall. The click-click-click morphed into scraping. Sharp edges dug into a surface not too far away from where Rel stood.

What the jiiq was that?

Rel's hands tightened around the figurine only to connect with the flesh of her palms. Where did it go? She searched for the shelf next to the fireplace. The other figurine had vanished.

The click-click-click started up again. This time it was behind her. Each click felt as if a wraith scratched along her spine spinning her around. The tiny edges of claws scoring her skin. She scanned the room, backing up as the clicking grew louder. Her hackles rising at the heavy breathing that joined it. Her nostrils flexed registering new scents. Dead meat with a hint of blood filled the warm moist air.

Drawing on her beast her vision washed red as she searched every corner of the room. Nothing. Not a hint of the energies she could normally detect when the strange cracks in the air appeared. What was more disturbing about the room was their absence. No cracks. No signs of the other world.

What the actual jiiq?

"Get out of there, Rel," A voice, softer than a whisper, surfaced amid the clicking, scratching, and heavy breathing. Rel's ears twisted, searching for the source.

"Hurry." The voice said.

Rel did an about face, dashing down the hall. Not excited about the option, but the hall led her away from the threat.

The breathing, clicking, scratching thing gained feet, which beat against the floor as it gave chase. Neither Rel nor her beast enjoyed running, but running meant survival or a chance at it. If anything, she would gain a little time. Time gave her a chance to strategize. As she pumped her legs, pushing her body to move faster, the doors she passed gained an appeal.

The thumping cadence of her pursuer shifted. A lighter, more rapid sound joined the morbid melody. The rhythmic pulsation of a heart.

"Hurry, Rel!" the voice encouraged. Its volume grew as she drew closer to the source. A dark blue door on her left. It moved in and out as if it were alive. The wood stretched enough to see a light inside between the narrow gap between the wall and the door.

Heavy breathing intensified. The warm flow of it prickled her flesh. What she needed was a weapon. She regretted her naiveté for following her mentor's advice. Weapons are useless in the

House of Testing. Some say that those who take them in have died by their own hand.

Rel opened and closed her hands, wishing for a blade. A blade would buy her time, or at least make her a threat to the thing pursuing her.

"In here!" The voice implored.

Rel didn't need to be told again as the weight of the thing chasing her filled the hall. Vibrations from the weight of its body escalated her need for safety. She grabbed the knob and tore the door open, darting inside just as the beast arrived. The door slammed shut but not before she caught a glimpse of what chased her. A slick black mass shaped like a were with claws as long as a sword. Its bulk bore the defining slopes of muscles and fur but the darkness cloaking it obscured its face. It noticed her looking and opened its mouth. A hole full of bold white teeth as sharp as Bharg spines, snapped at her. Light dissipated once the door shut. Only a thin line streamed in from the small space between the floor and the bottom of the door.

Rel lay on her back, held up by the backs of her arms. She reined in her breathing. Her heart still needed convincing that she was safe.

She pushed up, pulling her legs up to her chest, and listened. The thing outside lingered. She could tell from the shadow shifting along the small gap between the floor and the door. Its harsh breath pressed against the door followed by tapping.

Rel's ears twitched, angling to define the sound. It wasn't truly tapping, but something heavier, like the sharp end of an ax blade sinking into wood then yanked out.

The tapping gentled, becoming a series of scratches ending in silence. The breathing on the other side gained a rhythm to it. Heavy but calm.

Rel couldn't tear her eyes away from the dark blob at the center of the gap. Chest heaving. In the recesses of her mind her survival instincts screamed for her to move but she couldn't. Part of her wanted to know what lay on the other side. To see its face.

It was as if the thing outside read her mind because it slammed against the door. Her heart hammered inside her chest. Her body instinctively curled in a protective ball as she threw an arm up to shield her face. She braced herself for the inevitable impalement by debris from the splintering door.

Her breathing stopped. Reasoning kicked in after the creature rammed the door a third time and did not descend on her. Stretching out her limbs, Rel rose to her feet. The creature continued to slam against the door, but it did not give.

What was it?

Rafe said she would not die. Again, the creature slammed against the door. It did not jostle on its hinges nor did the wood crack. Fine white and gold particles shimmered at the core of the wood. They settled like wisps on the tip of a flower.

The pack's symbol took shape. Its presence stopped the creature's frenzy.

Tap-tap-tap.

Rel took an unconscious step forward, then stopped.

"Little wolf."

Tap-tap-tap.

"Little wolf."

Tap-tap-tap.

"Let me in."

Tap-tap-scratch.

Rel swallowed.

A thud against the door sent Rel scurrying back.

"Let me end your suffering."

It chuckled, then tapped again. Tapping morphed into a constant slow pounding broken by an ever-changing melodic request for Rel to let it in.

Rel waited. Years of managing bullies taught her to remain alert but silent. Listening and observing were her greatest weapon. Predators always showed themselves while bullies told on themselves. Which was the thing outside?

"What does the Mvunaji have to fear?" The creature said. Its words muted thunder as again, the sharp tips of claws sank into the door. "Are you not the harbinger of suffering masquerading as a healer?"

Rel swallowed. Her jaws twitched. The desire to snap at him, strong, but she did not speak. Instead, she needed to find a way out of this room. If she were lucky, she might find signs of the Hasking Stone, though she wasn't sure what to look for.

The creature's laughter shook the door on its hinges, though it was gentle. Something thumped against it.

"Why fight for them?" It said. "They are not deserving of mercy."

An image of Draega's twisted face and sharp tongue filled Rel's mind. Draega's venomous comments clogged her ears. Every word spoken as Rel worked to get her pup ready to travel. The malicious grin she flashed before bursting from the Commons to announce Rel's sin for the Mgwan's to hear. The image shifted, becoming a collage of Songga's stalking ending with Elias's mauling. Taunting voices closed in as the vision continued her story of abuse and rejection.

"Ungrateful dogs who shezia where they eat." It huffed. "What of your mother?" The thing clicked its tongue. "Poor, poor, Mother Farah. Her hands have healed many. What have the wolves done?"

Rel was so caught up in what the creature on the other side of the door was saying that she nearly missed the presence of another in the room with her. It was close.

She twisted her upper torso, keeping an eye on the door while her nose, ears and peripheral sight hunted for what hid in the darkness. Her pounding heart obstructed her breathing. The awkward rhythm of it dulled her hearing.

"Sihasin." A familiar voice called. It was faint. Softer than a whisper. Her ears twitched, searching for the speaker. Nothing.

"Sihasin." The word crackled in the air from all directions. It did this three times before revealing a point of origin. A piece of darkness broke apart from the rest as the word Sihasin echoed. Tiny lights sparkled in its wake. Illuminating the thing approaching her.

The creature in the hall began beating on the door in symphony with the approaching figure's steps.

"Sihasin." A slender lavender hued figure emerged from the darkness. Her healer's robes billowed behind her. Mother Farah clutched her hand which still bled. "Sihasin, look what they've done to me." Mother Farah lifted an unbandaged hand. The light in the room formed a halo around it, revealing two working fingers.

"Sihasin." Mother Farah's face was a mask of misery. "Look what they've done to me." She used her ruined hand to tug at the neckline of her tunic. Deep purple and black bruises decorated her collar bone.

"He will never keep his promise." Mother Farah moaned.

Rel took a step toward it. Pausing after her fifth step as she realized what she was doing. Mother Farah was on Blacktooth Land. In a dungeon within the Alpha's Fist. Rel backed away. Mindful of the illusion before her.

Mother Farah straightened. Her arms fell limp at her side. Misery melded into a toothy grin. Eyes glittering with mischief.

"The Blacktooth are not deserving of mercy." The thing wearing Mother Farah's face said. Disdain dripped from its words. It crept forward, remaining out of Rel's reach. Its face thoughtful as an idea brightened its expression.

"You should stop this." The fake Mother Farah's arms gestured toward the dark room. "End the trial here. Save yourself the heartbreak."

Rel blinked at it.

"What do you think will happen to me, win or lose?" A wicked smile lit up the fake Farah's face as she enthusiastically acted out several ways the alpha could kill her. "I'm dead." Fake Farah said, grabbing Rel by the shoulders. "I'm dead and you return to nothing."

Rel knocked the thing's hands away then shoved it. "As long as my family breathes, I will keep going!" Rel snarled.

Fake Farah lay on her back, body shaking with laughter. "Family." She rolled onto stomach pushing up on her elbows. "Family." Fake Farah said after the humor died.

"I'm not your family." Fake Farah stated dramatically dusting off her robes as she got to her feet. "You have no family."

Rel bristled. "Family is not about blood." Rel's beast roughened her voice. "Family is a collection of beings of a common heart and mind." She pressed her hand over her heart. "You are not my family."

Rel prowled closer to the Fake Farah. The scent of decay wafted through the darkness as the Fake Farah mirrored her movements.

"Pretty words." Fake Farah said. Her brilliant white healer's robes darkened into a deep red. "A salve to cover the ugliness of truth." Fake Farah sneered. Her elven face darkened, flickering between flesh and shadow. Dark purple eyes glowed amber as they danced.

"Pack is cruelty. Fake Farah's voice morphed into a guttural rumble. Her slender limbs thickened. Black patches mottled beautiful lavender skin. The dark patches moistened like blood as the body in front of Rel grew into the familiar creature that lurked outside.

Bold white teeth flashed. "Pack is suffering."

It swept forward. Rel turned, sprinting blindly into the pitch away from the taunting creature.

"The pack steals everything." The creature chanted behind her. "The pack lies."

A warbled squeak filled her with hope. Rel made a sharp right just as the creature lunged for her. The squeaky tempo crystalized joined by a gentle splash of water.

Home. It sounded like home.

Rel quickened her pace as she mentally batted away the creature's words. A short distance away, light collected revealing a doorway. Around its frame were symbols like the ones engraved in the trees around their property.

She reached for the doorway. The symbols burned bright revealing a whirlpool of colors. A kaleidoscope of red, green, blue, and silver. The light stretched toward her, and she reached for it.

Sharp claws sank into her shoulders just as the tips of her claws grazed the light's edge. Her back slammed against the creature behind her. Long ropes of darkness formed a curtain over her face as the creature bent over her.

Bold white teeth slashed across the enveloping darkness. “Remember Rel, mother’s lie too.” It whispered.

Rel’s mouth hurt as her jawbone cracked to make room for thicker, sharper teeth. The nailbeds at the end of her fingers bled as her claws lengthened. Her skin burned as her beast struggled to lay claim to her body in a shift.

The creature enveloping her chuckled at the beast trapped beneath her skin. Rel shoved her claws into the space inches away from its bold white teeth. Its laughter ended abruptly.

“You said it yourself.” Rel hissed as she pulled her claws from the sickly black essence. “Mother’s use pretty words to shield their children from ugly truths.”

It was her turn to flash a feral grin as the pressure of its body fell away. “A mother does what she must to preserve happiness of those she loves.” Rel glared at the mound of darkness. It spit gobs of sickly green and red ichor into the air. “My mother loves me. My family is worth fighting for.”

Rel resumed her flight. The slap of water against a water wheel pulled Rel closer to the colorful swirling lights. As she drew nearer, a long-ignored truth took root. For sixty-two years, she had believed she was immune to the nips of the pack’s slurs. She’d been diligent in the hardening of her heart, but every word the creature spoke chipped away at her armor.

Rel added power to her run as she embraced the meaning of Mother Farah’s secret name for her. Sihasin. It meant hope.

"You are Sihasin for yourself." Her mother would say, pressing a delicate finger in Rel's chest. "You are Sihasin to those you allow a place in your heart." Her mother would then touch the middle of Rel's forehead. "One day, you will be Sihasin to the pack."

Rel knew her mother's words were true but a tiny part of her didn't believe. A wave of shame washed through her as the truth bloomed. Rel passed through the cool colorful swirling light. Its intensity temporarily blinded her. Her feet tangled as she lost sight of the floor sending her falling face first onto the floor a familiar storeroom.

Chapter 24
Have a Heart

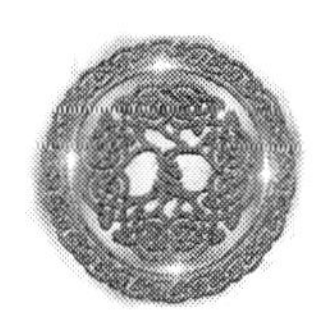

Dried meat, fruit, and polished wood filled the small room. Rel rolled onto unsteady feet. Her head pounding. She rubbed it as she tested the floor, pushing down on it using the balls of her feet.

It was solid.

Real.

She did a slow turn, inspecting her surroundings. Racks filled with sacks, jars, bowls, and boxes. She poked the bags, picked them up, and shook them. Their weight, smells, and the sound of what lay inside confirmed they were real, too.

Could it be she was back in the Commons? If so, had the testing already ended? Her brow furrowed as she searched her memory for the rules. Rafe said there would be six tests. Sometimes there were more.

She glanced at the door. It was like any door. Plain. Wooden. Rel walked over to it, looking down at the dull silver knob. If she turned it, would it open another portal?

Curiosity laid her palm against the smooth flat surface of the door. Its plainness drew her to press her ear against it. Outside was silent. She pressed her cheek into the wood, ears flexing in search of life. Her diligence was rewarded with whispers. They were faint. Distant. She wasn't alone.

She backed away, fingers flexing as she weighed her options. Was that creature with the bold white teeth lurking outside? Her impatience with mystery compelled her to turn the knob and push. The door swung open. A whitewashed stone wall with wood paneling in places greeted her. Voices rose and chairs scraped the floor. Whispers gained a rhythm as she stepped into the hall.

A light, as bright as the sun, obscured the activity beyond the mouth of the corridor. She cupped her hand over her brow as she made her way to the end of the hall. The light was constant, drawing her eyes to slits. Her red eyes preferred shadows. Light hurt them. Especially bright light. *Rel wore tinted veils during the daylight hours.*

"Check the barricades!" Old Elias barked. Furniture creaked and groaned in response.

Rel stepped into the brightness. Into the Greeting Hall. Light dimmed making it easier to see the wide archway and large windows. Blocked by mounds of furniture. Old Elias and several teenaged males tested the barricades. The frowns on their faces were concerning.

"Sihasin!"

Rel blinked against the burning light, ears swiveling, guiding her toward her mother's voice. She hoped the brilliance would wane as she followed the scent of infection and Candela Paste across the Greeting Hall into the Meeting Wing.

"My daughter is good with a needle. She will stitch you up quick with little to no pain." Her mother's pride swelled her heart. Rel tilted her head, nostrils flexed. Fragrant moon flowers, sweat, and medicine led her to the Stitching Room.

Rel found her, Dark purple curls were piled on top of her head, tied off with a strip of bandage as she knelt beside Alder. He lay on his side, eyes trained on her mother as she checked his stitches.

Rel found her mother hunched over the pup, Alder. Checking his wounds while lauding his bravery. Alder puffed out his chest, flinching quietly under Farah's probing hands. Rel strode over to her mother, choosing to stand behind her as she worked.

There felt as if she'd seen this before. Her mother, sorting through a set of five vials and a jar of Candela Paste. Farah pressed along the edge of the stich work. Speaking softly to him as she did. The wound was an angry red, though Rel had sterilized it before closing it. Candela Paste had been applied before Alder and his mother left for the Commons. Rel leaned over her mother's shoulder, inspecting her work. The stitching was tight. None of the flesh puckered. Why was it so red? There was no infection. She would have smelled it.

Something was wrong. She tapped her mother's shoulder, gesturing for them to trade places.

"Run!" Old Elias shouted, as an explosion rocked the Commons. Yelps and curses followed. Rel hurried from the Stitching Room, rounding the corner which led to the Greeting Hall. She expected to see a gaping hole but instead, furniture jostled but held firm.

Old Elias and the males flanking the entrance backed away. Weapons ready as they prepared to stand their ground.

Pups whined, holding tight to their mothers.

A second crash sent the able-bodied scattering. The barricade burst apart in the crash that followed. A loud boom accenting by cracking stone snatched screams from those too scared to run. A plume of thick gray dust spilled through the breach. It rolled into the hall in frothy waves.

"Get out!" Old Elias roared, raising his free arm to shield his face as the dust washed across the floor.

Quickly, the mass of wolves poured out of the Greeting Hall into the corridor leading to Alpha's Heart. The hall split near the end. Off to the left was a door which led to a narrow staircase. At the bottom was the Sorting Dock. The doors were heavier. If they were forced to take refuge there, at least there was food and water. Enough to feed the pack for a week. For those who made it out, there was the option of the Alpha's Fist or clusters of Cubbies set in the Wilds. If they were lucky, they might find a decent shelter.

Mothers and matrons used their bodies as barriers collecting along the lip of the hall. They picked through debris for suitable weapons. The elder matrons among them escorted the young. With all the commotion, Rel had yet to see her mother emerge from the Meeting Hall.

"Sihasin." Rel spun around. Her mother stood with Alder clutching her hand as the wounded gathered behind her. Rel jogged over, each step filling her with dread. She knew her mother. Knew what her mother would ask of her.

Rel shook her head before she could ask the question.

"Sihasin, it's our duty to keep them safe." Farah said, waving her hand toward the matrons gathering to fight. Farah grabbed Rel's shoulders, squeezed gently, and met her eyes. "We have to give them a chance," Farah said, glancing at the bodies filling the hall. A bellow drew every eye to the shape, forming as the gray cloud settled.

Songga Blackpaw strode through in his wehr form. Muzzle dripping with blood and spittle. Rel's breath caught in her throat as she waited for him to charge. He didn't. Crazed yellow eyes darted around the room.

A scrawny dark brown wolf Rel knew as Aylor, lunged forward on spindly legs. He brandished a jagged table leg. The wild splintered end aimed at Songga. Aylor stumbled past Songga who danced away from harm. His misstep cost him. As he fought to remain on his feet, Aylor's arms windmilled exposing his ribcage. Songga exploited the weakness, driving his claws into it. Impaling Aylor who managed a weak yelp before Songga extracted his heart.

"Get out!" Old Elias shouted before he surged forward, drawing back his short sword. Unlike Aylor, Old Elias was mindful of his opponent. He lacked speed but he knew how to bluff and where to strike. Killing Songaa was his mission. It was etched in his scowl.

Rel watched Old Elias nick a tendon in the arm Songga used to impale Aylor. Two moves later, sliced through the flesh of Songga's left knee. He failed to get the muscle he was after, but the snarl from the other wolf was reward enough. Staying out of Songga's reach, Old Elias tracked the younger wolf. They circled each other a dance of growls and clicking talon thick claws.

"Get them out of here, Sihasin." Farah said, drawing Rel's gaze away deadly waltz. "You have to lead them."

Farah did an about face and worked her way through the wounded, tapping those she passed urging them to follow Rel.

Rel found herself despising the quality in her mother that she most admired. The piece of her she spent a lifetime trying to emulate. Mother Farah's selfless nature. It was so contrary to the nature of beasts. Why couldn't she, just once, save herself. Wolves had fangs, claws, and sharp tongues. They lashed at their little family with vigor.

A soft tug of her half skirt. Rel looked down to see Alder, despite his wounds in euman skin. Her resentment dissipated. She liked the pup. Her attitude could get him killed. She didn't want him to die. If she was honest with herself, she didn't want the others to die either.

"Move!" Old Elias shouted as he and Songga toppled onto the floor. The momentum of their grappling bodies sent them sliding across it. Rel grabbed Alder, leaping out of the way. The fight shifted from the entrance to the corridor leading to the Alpha's Heart. Where their sliding bodies stopped.

Rel stood, setting Alder carefully on his feet. "We have to leave." She said, then turned to the wolves cowering beside her. "If you want to survive, we have to get out of here."

"Where can we go?" A male, a little older the Aylor asked. A single bright blue eye stared at her. The other was covered with bandages. Candela paste stained the bindings around his chest. He jerked his chin toward the writhing wolves.

Rel scanned the area, noting the hall from which she emerged when she first arrived was open. Before Mia, Rel never knew there was a hidden passage that led into the Forest of the Black Moon. Right now, it was their best option. If memory served her right. She'd left the door open.

Rel kept her eyes on the Old Elias and Songga while signing her plan to the group. The wolves who could, shifted into their euman forms. Padding quietly by. There were so many wounded, it would be impossible for her to guard them all.

Rel snapped her fingers. The crowd of wolves froze. "I need a few of you to guard our flank."

Seven peeled away and joined her at the mouth of the corridor. More began working their way toward her. She stopped them. "Keep the rest of the pack safe."

Their heads bobbed in agreement as they positioned themselves outside the flow of bodies. Their eyes were watchful. Ushering stragglers along.

A gentle tug of her hand pulled her focus to the little wolf clasping it. Alder's wide eyes filled with questions. Fear floated on the tears welling in them. She crouched beside him, pulling him to her side. Her ears swiveled, one remained aimed at the snarling snapping wolves and the other tilted toward the pup.

"I'm scared." He whispered.

"I know." Rel met his gaze. She stroked his face. "I'm scared too." She replied.

His brows knit together; his eyes darted away. He stared at his feet, his wolf ears spread, curling toward her words. "But you're Mvunaji. Why would you be scared?"

Rel leaned in, as if sharing a secret. "Even Mvunaji feel fear."

Alder considered her words. He plucked the hem of her half skirt. His shy gaze flitting between her face the stream of wolves passing through the hall.

"What do you do?" He whispered.

Rel untangled his hand from her skirt and held them between hers. She inched closer and said, "I keep going."

"Even if you're scared?" Alder's awed whisper rose.

Rel nodded.

"Why?"

"If I stay still, the thing I'm scared of will catch me."

Alder contemplated her words.

"Alder, you have to go." She pleaded with the pup. Old Elias yelped. Startling them all. Rel covered Alder's eyes as fresh blood christened the air. He didn't need to see Old Elias die. His body writhing under the weight of Songga. Songga pinned Old Elias, his teeth embedded in the back of his throat. There were bite marks and bits of missing flesh on Elias's ravaged body. His teeth gnashed in a snarl; golden-brown eyes defiant as his wolf stared defiantly at his killer.

Rel kept her hands over Alder's eyes as she steered him toward the others.

"Don't make me go." He pleaded, stiffening his legs, making it harder for Rel to move him.

"You can't stay." Rel said, his reluctance forced her to carry him.

"But I'm by myself." He whispered. Uncertainty weighed his words.

"The pack is your family." It felt strange to say, but the approaching matron confirmed her statement. "Which means we're family." The pup smiled.

"You're my sister, right." He asked in an excited whisper.

Rel confirmed their bond with a nod.

The elder female dressed in a simple yellow tunic dress collected him.

"You're coming too?" Alder asked, his hand darted out, snagging Rel before he settled in the matron's arms.

"Later," she said. Again, unraveling his fingers. "Honest." She lied. Content with the hope rising in his eyes.

"Come little, one," the matron urged, taking a firm grasp of his hand. Alder cast one last look at Rel before vanishing around the corner.

"Thank the goddess." She whispered to herself. The stillness in the room alerted her to the battle's end.

The click-click-click of claws upon the barren floor turned her around. Songga loomed a short distance away. Close enough to reach her should he be inclined to do so, but far enough away, that Rel believed she might get away, should she run.

His lips peeled back, flashing bloodstained teeth.

"My prize." He purred. Hot breath warmed the crown of her head.

She looked up, noticing a gaping hole where his heart was supposed to be. She reached for it, and he let her. Songga remained motionless as he did. She laid her hand over his right peck. Far enough away from the ruined bits near the gap. It pulsed. Thumped as if a heart still lived there.

Songga was dead. She'd killed him.

She pulled her hand away, but Songga snared it. Covering it with his large meaty one. His cool flesh bothered her.

"I don't care that you took it.". Songga said, flashing bloodstained teeth. His eyes were as lively as rocks as looked their fill. "It belonged to you." He chuckled, adding pressure to Rel's captured hand.

What was she supposed to do? She could fight him, but how could she kill what was already dead?

Songga pressed harder. Pain shot down her arm, pooling at the elbow. The hole in his chest thumped with more vigor. His bloodstained grin stretched.

"Let go of my sister!" Alder's shriek shattered Songga's menace. He sprinted toward them, holding his side. His eyes glowed amber as he attempted to shift. Fur spread along his limbs as they extended. They tangled as he ran, sending him crashing to the ground.

Songga laughed. A deep ragged bellow as the pup rolled awkwardly. His body caught in the throes of a shift.

"What did I promise?" Songga leaned in. Rancid breath activated her gag reflex. "I would kill those who want what is mine."

He released her and charged toward the still rolling pup. Fear and rage devoured her as Songga closed the distance between him and Alder. Her world splintered. Thin cracks shattered the space around her. Calling. Beckoning her to dive inside.

Rel's instinct was always to avoid them, but the urgency of the situation pushed her inside. Warm orange light swallowed her. Inside the fissure was a short tunnel. She could see Alder at the other end. A distorted shadow lingered at her back. Rel raced to Alder, leaping from the orange tunnel, snatching up the pup. She cradled him to her chest just as something pierced it.

"Jiiq." Songga growled. "I told you they weren't worth saving." He said, as he removed his hand from Rel's chest.

She slumped forward, still clutching Alder. He was quiet as her grip on him eased. His body melded into its natural state. A four-legged werewolf pup slipped from her grasp. Rel wanted to touch him. Test his vitals for life.

Her chest burned in the spot where Songga pierced it. Had she failed them. Failed Alder. Her mother. The pack? Was it over?

Her vision darkened. The room became a pair of dark tunnels. Her sight phased in and out with every blink. She could only see what was above her. Her lips twitched. Was she frowning? Songga loomed at the end of the twin tunnels. She hated the view.

Rel wondered if she could take him with her to the Deadlands. He cradled her in his arms like she was something precious. She coughed. It was wet. The burning spread, joined by knives that slashed along her throat and chest. She was dying.

Growls, barks, and howls filled Rel's ears. Rel was soon pried from Songga's grasp and laid on the ground. Her darkening vision caught glimpses of the wolves who fled. The seven who volunteered to defend the pack flashed across her line of sight. Hushed voices cushioned her as drops of water splashed on her face.

Was it raining?

Her breathing slowed in the absence of her heart. She needed a new one, if she was going to fulfill her mother's wish. Rel's sense of smell dulled along with her sight. She hoped to see her mother before it failed her.

It seemed to be the will of Luna, to grant Rel one last look at her mother. She appeared at the end of the shrinking points of sight.

"Sihasin." Her mother said, scooping Rel into her arms. Rel's body flopped as Farah adjusted her grip. "Sihasin." She moaned. Her breath brushing against Rel's ears.

Rel attempted to speak, but her mouth refused.

Her mother hugged her tighter. Rel's ears brushed her lips.

"What is the pack?" Her mother whispered.

The pack is neither pawn nor prey, but family. Her spirit responded.

"Very good, daughter." Luna murmured against her cheek.

A swirl of colorful lights swirled over Rel. The dark tunnels of her sight expanding. She felt something rise from the floor. Air crackled. Lightning popped and flashed at the edge of her vision. The goddess lifted her in her arms and carried her through the portal. Each step the goddess took restored Rel's senses.

Fertile soil, sap, and fragrant flowers slipped into her nostrils. Her chest remained still. The fire in it dulled. Maybe it was the draft coursing through the hole in it as the goddess strode through the Forest of the Black Moon. Rel was placed on a hard surface where she lay staring up through a canopy of black and green leaves. Perfect round silver and blue moons looked down on her. Frayed clouds marred the perfect night.

The goddess lay her hand beside Rel's wound. She held up a red pearl. Rolling it between her fingers, she angled it to catch the moon's rays. A grim line shaped her lips as she pushed the red pearl into the gap. A wild flutter pulsating as the pearl settled into the gap. Bone and sinew knit together until the wound was gone.

"Rest daughter, as your heart settles." The goddess said as she stroked Rel's arm. "You'll need it for what's to come."

Luna's eyes faded from sight, as Rel slept, and her body healed.

Chapter 25
Smoke Signals

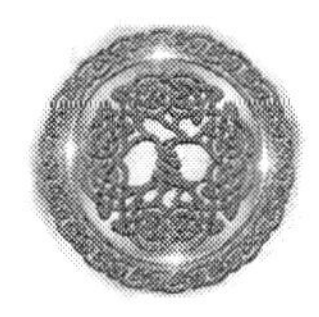

Rel blinked. Her staggered breaths set the dragon's breath pollen to glow. A mound of black petals flickered in front of her. She gazed around. Long-weathered necks of trees formed a curtain beside the hard surface she slept on. Rel winced as she sat up. Her bones were not pleased with how she slept. Muscles screamed as she stretched. The tightness in them ebbed as she curled her body toward the sky.

Bugs serenaded the night and from the look of the trees, she was in the Forest of the Black Moon. Fear was not a constant thing for Rel, but she could not ignore the rising dread within her. The presence of black trees and the single silver eye of Luna worried her. She dragged her hands along the stone beneath her. Her fingers traced the beveled grooves of a carving she was intimately familiar with. Luna!

Rel flipped over to get a better look at what she was sitting on. The hollows of Luna's she-wolf flowed across the stone. Rel was in the Arms of Luna.

Was she dead?

She searched her memory, recalling how she lost her heart. Frantic hands felt along the bone above her left breast. There was no stiffness in the fabric. She pressed her chin to her throat. Moonlight touched the surface of the stone under her. It gathered like water in the engraving. Particles of light drifted up like pollen. It was bright enough for Rel to discern the absence of blood. The fabric of her fitted shirt was still intact. Her hand shifted down, covering her left breast, where a strong heart pulsated against her palm.

A relieved sigh shattered the forest song. She rocked, grateful she lived, but ashamed that her terror made her forget why she was there. The Hasking Stone. Never once during the challenge had she searched for the Hasking Stone. What was the point of enduring such horror if there was no prize?

Bugs quieted. Rel's ears instantly searching for intruders. The lack of a breeze didn't help. She pushed forward onto her stomach and crawled across the altar. If wolves paced below the height of the altar coupled with darkness should conceal her. Most wolves wouldn't stare too long for fear of Gwyl. He escorted the deceased to the Deadlands, where they would be sent on their eternal paths. Warriors and good men dwelled in Gwyl's hunting grounds where they would feast or hunt. While wicked wolves would spend an eternity as prey. Forever hunted by Gwyl and his spectral hounds.

Rel shivered whenever she thought of the hounds. It was said that they could pass through dimensions ahead of their prey. Their bark was loudest when they were far away. To hear it meant death was near. Gwyl was coming. Rel looked across the Forest of the Black Moon. A smattering of Stars dotted the sky casting a pale blue aura across the treescape reminding Rel that the land was sacred. Even Ulmer's Fangs respected Luna's territory. Mindful of Gwyl.

Rel hesitated at the edge unsure of what she would find below. Would there be more monsters, like the beast with the bold white grin or would there be an endless abyss. She inhaled a deep fortifying breath before she poked her head over the altar's edge. An abyss hid the ground. Bits of moonlight shaped the base of trees and the curve of leaves but there were no signs of life. Rel backed away from the edge, scooting until her hip brushed the mound of glowing back petals.

Was she dead? The question burned as she scanned her surroundings. The darkness seemed to shift. It thickened. She counted the trees, taking note of how far they went. Seven layers were visible.

A soft click of claws spun her around. Her place on the altar shifted. She sat in the center. The mound of black petals blazed. Rel moved her hand close. Fire licked the space near her fingers as she quickly pulled back, scanning the surrounding darkness.

Seeing nothing though her ears flicked and twisted, and her eyes narrowed. Something was out there.

Tap. Tap. Tap.

Jiiq! It was back!

A lethargic scratch of talon thick claws emanated directly across from her. The tapping accelerated. Sparks flared in the pocket of darkness where it hid. Habit sent her hands in search of a weapon. Smooth, cool stone answered.

Shezia! Rel rolled onto all fours. Muscles coiled to pounce. Bones along the length of her spine crackled as the beast beneath her skin stretched. Her nail beds bled, making room for her lengthening claws. Gums itched and burned as her teeth thickened. The cartilage along of her nose throbbed. Her face adapted to larger teeth and lupine nose. Her vision adjusted to the darkness. She glared at a red blob. Sparks from its tapping claws constricted her pupils.

"Show yourself," Rel demanded. She was proud of the firmness in her voice. Her fluttering heart knocked against her breastbone. She pushed air from her nostrils, offering a prayer to the goddess as she braced for an attack.

This was a test. It had to be because the shapeless thing across from her was not real.

It moved.

Rel tracked it. The red, formless blob stretched. Every step its shape defined. Songga stepped from the shadows. Smooth brown skin wrapped tight over unending muscle. He donned a loincloth and nothing else. A dark red scar blazed across his left peck marred perfection. A subtle flex of her nostrils returned no scents. Salt paired with Songga's natural musk should have colored the air, but there was nothing. The atmosphere was dormant. Dead. Again, making her wonder if her condition was the same.

Songga sat, legs crossed, with his hands on his knees beside the burning petals. His eyes were dark caverns. Not a speck of white. He stared at her. She stared back. Neither of them said a word.

The soft slap of pacing feet rose behind her. Her position on the altar shifted, pushing her closer to the wall of darkness. It felt thicker. She reached for it but at the last minute she stopped herself. The patter of pacing feet grew louder. Clearer. Closer. Rel felt the brush of wind generated from her mother's pacing. She leaned into it, nostrils flexing in the hopes of catching her scent.

"I worry about her." Her mother's voice swirled in the space around her head.

"What mother does not worry about her child?" Mia, the matron who helped Rel flee, answered.

"He will expel her from the pack if she does not prove her worth," Mother Farah sighed.

"But she has," Mia said. Her voice rising as Mother Farah's faded. "She saved the pup and his mother."

Farah dismissed Mia's words with the wave of her hand, looking off at the cell's interior wall.

Silver gray mists ascended from the platform. As it took shape, Songga faded beneath it. In his place, her mother and Mia sat together. Farah was in a cell cradling her injured hand in her lap. Mia sat on the steps beside it. It was a replay of her mother's memory. Rel sat somewhere in the ether, close enough to hear and see them.

"I love my daughter, but she has a penchant for destruction," Farah said. "That temper of hers has created more work for me."

Mia's laughter took to the air like startled wisps. It fluttered around her head, popping like bubbles as it died.

Rel's a child. Mia said. *She's your child.*

Farah rubbed her flat stomach, head shaking as worry etched across her face. *She's a promise I must keep.*

Mia inched closer to Farah, reaching through the bars, intent on comforting her friend, but Farah distanced herself.

You've done your part, made things right. Mia said, gripping the bars. *She's a healer, like you.* Mia rapped her knuckles on the bars. *Like her mother.*

The altar shifted. Its sudden motion making Rel dizzy. Her dizziness passed quickly. She found herself perched on the step beside Mia.

Is she though? Farah's bitter skeptical words burned Rel's ears. She watched her mother change as she turned hard lavender orbs on her friend.

I'm not her mother. Farah's words were sharp, sinking like teeth into Rel's heart. *She's a foundling dropped in my lap by the gods.* Farah inched closer, sticking her good hand through the bars.

Rel shifted on the step, wanting to get up and run but her need to know kept her what she was, where she came from anchored her.

She's my chance. Farah rubbed her ruined hand across her knee. Blood tainted the air, marring the odor of moon flowers and healing herbs. *My chance to atone for the lives lost because of me.*

Those deeds are from another time. They died with Chindi. Mia pressed her head to the bars. Farah mirrored her action.

"I died." Farah knocked her ruined hand on her chest. "But this soul's still the same." Farah looked away from Mia. Away from Rel. The scent of moon flowers and medicine washed through the atmosphere. Its spark nipped at the fine hairs on Rel's skin as a soft lavender light surrounded her mother's body.

"I promised him." The glow intensified as Farah spoke. "Take care of the pack. Keep them safe."

"Promised who?" Mia said, drawing up, head and ears twitching in a wave of confusion.

"Chindi. Ulmer." Farah said. "My life for a favor."

"Rel is the favor?" Shock laced Mia's words.

Farah nodded and Rel's heart shattered.

"You love her. "Mia's words were firm but unsure.

"I bartered with Ulmer so I could raise her." Farah clutched her chest; fresh blood stained the bandages. Her aura brightened. Tendrils of light wrapped around her wrists. "If I didn't love her, why would I deny the greatest part of me?" Magic flared.

"Why here? Why raise her here?" Mia asked.

"A promise." Farah shrugged.

"To Ulmer?" Mia gaped at her friend. "He's a dog. A rabid one at that."

Farah shook her head and said, "Not him." Her magic fell away from Farah. She pointed at the mark on her head. A scythe blade with a moon at its center. Rel bore the same mark, but hers was over her heart.

Mia's eyes grew wide. "Oh, goddess."

"I would guard what was his in exchange for my life." Farah said, her lips curved in a wistful smile. "Who would have thought my fear of death would deliver to me my greatest joy?"

Rel's head ached. Words. Pretty words mixed with barbs. What was true? Rel stared at the being she called mother. She looked the same, but she was different. A stranger. This stranger was why she came willingly to Elderton. Why she entered this house? At the end of this test, their little family was supposed to go back to how it was. Her father would return, and Ulmer would leave them alone.

Tufts of darkness swirled around her feet as she laughed at the absurdity of her childish desires. Who was she to hope for happiness? Peace? The darkness congealed.

"Declarations of love. Sweet names. Smiles." Songga said. His warm breath darkened the vision. Restored the shadows, wiping away the traces of her mother and Mia.

Warm skin pressed against her back. Ropes of black hair cascaded across her shoulder. Lush lips and a jaw dusted with spikes of stubble scraped her temple.

"Poor, poor, Mvunaji." Songga's warm breath caressed her face. "I told you mother's lie."

Hurried feet slapped against the stone. Close. The runner remained concealed in shadow.

"Parents keep secrets to save their young." A female said. The voice was familiar to Rel, but she couldn't recall a name.

Songga chuckled. His arms coiled around Rel's shoulders and chest. Her elbows grazed his inner thighs.

"Mother's lie to save their own skin," Songga replied.

Rel could feel the slow roll of his eyes toward the speaker in the shadows.

"She is not yours!" Farah screamed at Songga.

Rel's head hurt. It felt like a blade chipping away at the top of her skull. The truth of what Songga said add to the sharpness settling behind her eyes.

Farah stepped from the shadows a vaporous apparition. "She is Sihasin." Farah said, the fingers of her good hand clutching the fabric of her shift. "She's my daughter."

Songga's laughter vibrated against Rel's back. "She's a chip you used to bargain for a second life." Songga spit the words like venom. His grip on her tightened.

Rel waited for her mother to counter what Songga said. She sank a little deeper into despair. Soft fabric brushed against her shins. Rel opened her eyes. She didn't recall closing them.

"Sihasin." Farah kneeled before her child. "Sihasin, you know I love you."

Rel flinched.

Farah reached for her, but Songga snarled and she backed away.

"I'm a tool," Rel said. Her words were dagger sharp. "Everyone wants something from me."

"No," Farah denied. Beautiful. Graceful Farah. Liar.

"I am a silon." Rel said, her fingers wrapping around Songga's arms. "A thing used for trade." The charms on Rel's collar glowed.

"You don't understand what was sacrificed to give you this life." Farah reached for Rel again. Songga batted away her hand away, pulling Rel closer, deeper into him and stopped. He rested his chin on her head.

"Sacrifice," he said, smacking his lips, then clucked his tongue. "You've gained a full life." Songga's embrace tightened around Rel, but it wasn't uncomfortable. It was more like sinking into water.

Songga rubbed the length of Rel's forearms. "Little wolf." His words were gentle and sweet. "Always a pawn," his voice rumbled, tickling the skin of her shoulders and hips. "I would have given you all of Blacktooth. Spilled the blood of those who would dare break your heart." His legs shifted, drawing up as Rel sank deeper into the warm, rumbling body. "As my mate, not as a puppet."

"You're rabid, Songga," Rel said. Her words slurred. She wanted to look up at him. The monster who darkened her world but couldn't. "Rabid things bite. They kill."

Songga chuckled. His embrace tightened. Rel sank further into him. "So, I like to kill. Bloodletting draws out poison. Death makes room for the birth of new things." Songga looked down at her, which seemed impossible. He was so high up. There was something strange in his eyes. Madness? Affection?

"What is Mvunaji with his scythe," he replied. "Without his messenger to announce his coming?"

"Nothing," Rel said, sinking further into the abyss of Songga's body.

A luminous white arm darted out, latching onto the bottom of Rel's leg and pulled. Rel looked down at it. Gawking at the blood red hand wrapped around her shin.

"Let go, child." The voice was deep though the arm was slender. Feminine. It rang in her head. The strangeness of it chased away Rel's lethargy.

"Why," Rel countered.

"Let go," the voice persisted.

Songga's arms constricted. Rel winced at the sudden crack along her breastbone.

"Why?" Rel asked again. The inside her chest felt like it was leaking.

"Remember why you're here," the voice insisted.

"I'm here because I killed the only wolf who told me the truth," Rel said, brows arching at the roughness of her words.

She coughed. Something popped. A squelching like meat being torn from the ligament of bone. Rel bent at the waist. A sharp pain lanced along her ribs, ending under her armpit.

"Let. Him. Go," the stranger pleaded.

"Do you want me to forget what she said," Rel snapped. Her words dug into her chest and throat like Bharg spikes. A fit of coughing overtook her but she would say her piece. "Ignore truth." Her eyes watered. "No one keeps what they don't want!"

Something wet spilled from her mouth, coating her lips with every word she spoke.

A familiar face entered the void. A she-wolf in euman form. Not the goddess from the gates, but one she'd glimpsed whenever she visited the Forest of the Black Moon. Luminous skin and hair seemed to hold the glow of the moon. But her hands and the tips of her ears and hair were like Rel's, a deep crimson red. The part of the she-wolf that struck Rel was her eyes. They mirrored her own.

"Let it go," the she-wolf said. Her voice was as deep as a male. She recognized its cadence.

"You want me to forgive her?" Rel shot back. She imagined her voice was punishing, but her words barely registered in her ears.

"The pack isn't worth your life, little wolf," Songga whispered in Rel's ear.

"Let. It. Go," the she-wolf urged.

Rel kicked at her until her leg was free.

Songga's embrace became crushing.

"No," Rel whispered and was swallowed into the void. Veins of colorful light flowed around her as Rel descended. Death wasn't so bad, she thought, as the sound of a door swinging open filtered through her thoughts.

Maybe she was the fool, after all, for believing distance and separation kept her safe. Her belief that her home with Farah, Grace and her father was paradise. The illusion that she was loved. Important. Being born strange served a purpose. That *she* was Sihasin. Hope.

A lie.

All of it a lie.

Truth was a fire. It burned as the colors surged around her. The collar around her neck became a torment. Collecting the heat engulfing her. Rel tore at it. Relief cooling the burn as the collar fell away.

Why did she hurt? Why were the monsters the only beings in her life that were honest. Claws. Darkness. Blades from her broken heart cut her to pieces and for the first time in sixty-two years Rel howled.

Chapter 26
Bitter Words and Bickering Brothers

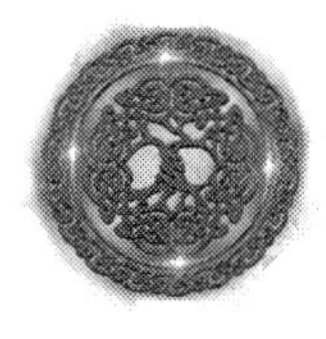

Groans filled the Commons with the red crystal hovering above their heads.

"She's dead," someone wailed.

"She's not," said another. "The stone would be black if she died."

"What if she gave up?" Tula, the matron who managed the Scout said. She pushed away from the wall near an overturned serving island. "I would have given up before I set foot on the island."

Growls erupted.

Ashera pounded on the table where she sat. "Deplus! The lot of you." She said, swinging an accusing finger around the room. "You've been fatus and dicks to Rel and my master, always." Ashera huffed, shooting up from the table, nearly knocking it over.

"Like you're innocent." A female with pale brown hair and skin chided. Her orange tunic dress swished as she strode over to confront Ashera. She stood in front of the larger female, sizing her up in a glance. "What makes you so righteous?"

Ashera shoved the smaller female, knocking her to the floor. She was on her, claws at her throat and teeth bared. "I learned. I went to my master on my own and learned. I saw her kindness. I treasure it." Ashera leaned in. "I protect it."

Ashera squeezed the small female's throat before releasing her to stand. "Mother Farah and Rel should be treated as pack."

"They're not wolves, so they are not pack," the small female hissed as she rolled onto her stomach and pushed up to stand on unsteady feet. She rubbed her neck while scowling at Ashera. "She offered up your son to the goddess's pyre."

"She gave him a beautiful passing. Even when his sickness was at its worst. She took away his pain. Gave him peace." Ashera's lip curled. "Unlike you," she snarled, eyes searching the faces for challenge. "Before Mother Farah, you walked across the sick. You let them die."

"Sick wolves are a weakness," an elder male said. He was hidden behind a crowd of wolves in wehr form along the front of the Greeting Hall.

"Rabid words from a rabid wolf," Ashera spat. She was so tired of cowards wrapping themselves in lies.

"Our alpha broke the curse," the elder counted bravely, yet he did not step forward.

"Did he really," Ashera countered and gestured around the room. "This is the blessing," she felt her wolf climb her limbs. It sat behind her eyes. She didn't let it surface fully. As a euman she could speak her piece. As a wolf, it would tear through as many as she could. The wolves surrounding her were proud cowards. Muzzled in the alpha's laws. They saw the truth but denied it. "Our pups are taken away from us. We are fed to our own pack. Why!"

"It's our way," the elder said again. His words were frail. "We are pack. We make sacrifices."

"What is pack, anyway?" Ashera countered. "We're prey animals hunted by the one who is supposed to guide us."

"Rel is an abomination. If she dies, she dies," another wolf said. "Preferably after the House of Testing."

"It's the will of the goddess to purge her from our number," the elder chimed in. His tone was sure.

"Like it is the alpha's will to sacrifice us to his adopted sons." Ashera barked. "We deserve to be cursed."

"Watch your tongue!" Bren said.

"Why? Did any of you watch yours when you hurled insults at the pack's champion?" Ashera folded her arms, daring them to contradict her.

"She was meant for sacrifice," Bren said, striding toward Ashera. He was a Scout. His merchant smile in place. "She is the speckled Bleet our ancestors would have offered to Gwyl before going to war."

A snarl built in Ashera's throat. "Jiiq you, you pompous plu. She's not a silon." Ashera gestured to the red Hasking Stone. "If you don't have a heart, consider your pockets. What's the curse going to do to your coin?"

Bren huffed, but Ashera enjoyed the fear in his eyes. He pulled on his robes, huffed again, then strode away.

"Has anyone ever considered." Ashera tapped her finger to her temple, her voice escalating in volume. "That the testing is not only for our champion, but us."

Ashera went over to the table she abandoned, collected her healer's bag, and left the room. She could at least carry on her master's work. Part of her wished she wasn't a werewolf because the ones in the room she left behind were stupid, heartless, and full of jiiq.

Red stained the walls of the Hasking Room. Rafe pressed his head against the glass in front of him.

"No!" Rafe said, his hand weakly smacking the glass. "Why wouldn't you listen?" His rubbed the goddess's brand. He didn't like the numbness.

"You should have let it go," he chanted, his hand sliding down the glass.

"We're not the forgiving type," Ulmer said.

Rafe stiffened. He watched his brother's reflection. Ulmer did not approach him but lingered off to his right. He sat on the arm of the closest bench.

"She'll win," Ulmer said. The confidence in his voice rankled.

"How do you know that?" Rafe turned, his hip punished him for the move. "She's had no time to train." Rafe's annoyance ebbed. He's spent the seven years on Farah's land training Rel. Their talks. The chores. The quiet excursions through the Deadlands. Their hunts. He taught her how to walk among wolves. How to read them. Fight them as needed. "Why should she put in the effort to win?"

Ulmer held up a crimson stained sack. "She'll do anything to save her mother."

"We don't know what the House of Testing will show her," Rafe said, willing himself to remain where he was. All his soul wanted to tear into his brother, but now was not the time. Rel needed him. There was a chance she might reach out to him. He had to be ready.

"I made it through with no guidance," Ulmer said, pride dripping from his statement. "I've watched her over the years." He began pacing. "She's strong," he said, pivoting away from his brother.

He walked over to the Hasking Room door, his hand on the knob. Looking over his shoulder affectionately at his distraught sibling. "I'll make her my daughter when she returns." He pulled open the door and shrugged. "I might even make that witch my bride." His wistful words pushed his mouth into a delighted smile.

Rafe stared at the door long after his brother's departure. He'd see Ulmer dead before he let him take his family, but first he had to save them. For now, he had to trust Mia to carry out her part while Ulmer's eyes were fixed on the Commons.

Mia in the Wilds where the Longtooth exist. She enters an encampment. The message in her pocket burns her palms. They vowed to only follow an alpha of the old ways. Cannot protect those who submit themselves to perversion. A series of questions bring them out.

"The pack needs its teeth," Mia spoke, feeling silly as she stared at the trees. Wings flapped overhead, dislodging a few leaves. Her ears flickered, searching for the panting of wolves, the crunch ofleaves and dead branches underfoot. Where were the y?

She tried again.

"A wolf without teeth has no hope," she called, turning slowly in the clearing.

"Our teeth serve only those willing to bear their own," a gruff voice resounded.

Mia waited. Hoping the wolf would approach.

"A wolf near death will embrace anything to survive," Mia responded. Something moved at the edge of her range of sight. The need to protect her back was strong, but did not move.

"Sick wolves are put down and the dead burn," the wolf said.

Mia felt him moving among the trees. He wasn't alone. Another lingered nearby.

"Longtooth vowed to keep watch over Luna's pack," Mia kneeled, head bowed as running feet approached. Branches snapped. Growls filled the air. She gathered her courage as it drew closer. "The Longtooth have failed their goddess."

Rancid wet breath rained on Mia's face as a huge black wolf snarled. It snapped its teeth. She jerked away.

"Where is the honor of the Longtooth?" Mia continued as the wolf in front of her yipped and growled. Several more joined it. All of them were larger than Ulmer's Fangs. "Your sons and daughters are stolen. Taught to hunt their own while you hide here in the Wilds."

A pair of wolves nipped at Mia. Their teeth cut her skin. Nothing deep.

"How dare you," the black wolf in front of her shifted into his euman form. A large male with skin the same hue as his fur stood before her. His hair was a shadow, black with strands of gray. Amber eyes glaring down as Mia raised her head and did a foolish thing. She flashed her teeth. Dark brown eyes burned amber.

"Hello Ok'r," she said, lifting her palm to expose the black crescent moon at its center. Symbols. The old language filled it. "Or should I say, grandfather?"

The wolf standing over her swallowed.

"You are blood," the wolf said. "I can offer you safety, but I will not defend toothless creatures." He stomped away from Mia into the trees. The wolves that had gathered around her disperse.

"You kill your own kin, Ok'r." Mia shouted. Ok'r froze.

"We keep our kin," Ok'r tossed over his shoulder.

"Lies," Mia rose. "The Longtooth are not the honorable dogs of the goddess," her words echoed in the vastness of the trees. "You allow her children to be tortured. Twisted into objectionable beasts. Wolves not worthy of their creature."

She stomped toward her grandfather. "The pack's shame belongs to the goddess." Her grandfather stiffened, fists curling as a growl rumbled in his chest.

"Our shame is your shame," Mia hissed. "A shame the Longtooth have allowed to befall the goddess."

Wolves stalked from the shadows surrounding her. They yipped and snarled but did not bite. She reached into the pocket of her skirt for the message she came to deliver.

"It's no wonder the pack has forgotten you." Mia tossed the paper at him. It fell to the ground. Growls resurrected. Mia let her wolf show, bearing her own teeth at the wolves surrounding her.

"I bite back," she snarled.

"Leave her be," Ok'r stood behind her. The wolves quieted, turned and trotted into the forest. "Follow me, child," he said, waving the folded paper aloft. "We'll talk at my camp."

Ok'r shifted into a black wolf before dashing into the forest. Mia adjusted the straps of her pack, then shifted into a gray wolf and followed. Praying to Luna as she ran that the Longtooth would rise and lend their teeth to the pack.

Chapter 27
Of the Same Mind and Body

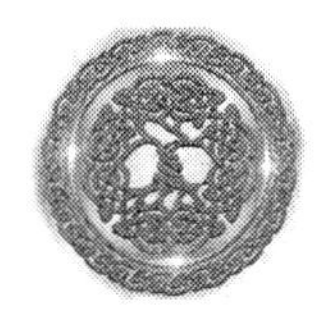

"It's time," someone whispered, sounding more feline than euman.

Rel opened her eyes to a familiar darkness. A stench soaked the spot where she lay. Her hands flexed and straw poked into her palms. Where was she?

She blinked, wetting her eyes. Another blink sharpened her vision. A Kalika lightly slapped her face. Snow white fur gleamed in the firelight. Its black, orange, and brown spots melded in a frown at the center of its forehead. A glossy pale blue collar around its neck.

Rel's groggy brain wondered why it was with her. Kalikas rarely ventured beyond the Wilds. They fed on moonlight, which gave their fur a constant glow. Rel knew of them because they traded with her mother for medicines and moon flowers. They used them for rituals and decorations. Their magic was coveted by many, which was why they lived in the Forest of the Black Moon. The Wilds hid away outcasts. Hid away deadly things. Some without names.

"Quickly," the Kalika urged, slipping her arm under Rel's armpits. "We don't have much time." It lifted her up, small triangular ears flat on its head as the brief slashes over its brow pulled in as she tied a sash around her waist.

Rel grunted as her body, which felt heavy, wobbled in its ascent. Another pair of hands grabbed her shoulders to keep her from falling.

"The den mother has marked the trail for you," the female behind her whispered. Her round belly soothed the ache in Rel's back.

"What about you? Aren't you coming, Viiya?" the Kalika whisper shouted.

"I can't," Viiya said, her hand pressed against her belly. "I'm too close. My baby will not let me make the run."

"But..."

"We don't have time." Viiya was resolute in her reply. "All of us will make it, be it in this life or the next."

Rel felt a gentle shove.

"We made a pact, remember? Escape or die," Viiya said. "Both are a mercy for our little ones."

The Kalika holding Rel upright led her from the dark room. No, not a room, but a prison cell. They passed a collection of them. Most were empty, but a few were occupied. Inside them were creatures she'd only heard about from Scouts or her mother. A variety of shifters: feline, lupine, serpent, and avian. There were a few species that looked like they did not have a euman form at all. Their bodies seemed too big and too different to phase into a something delicate.

"Wait here." The Kalika's warm breath grazed her scalp. She propped Rel against something solid as she approached a mirrored wall. The Kalika felt along the sides while Rel stared at her reflection.

A pregnant lupine female stared back from within the mirror. Gone was Rel's umber skin with patches of white on her face, legs, and arms. The reflection had white skin with red hands, ears, and feet. Her reflection had ears like Rel, tipped with crimson. The only difference was both were white instead of one white and one brown.

Rel lifted her hand. Her reflection did the same, dragging the tips of red-tipped fingers along the outer curve of the ear to its tip. She flicked the silver chains, enchanted by their delicate song. They were as thin as thread. They linked from an ornamental obsidian stud near the tip, ending at a matching septum ring bearing a silver bead at its center. Rel's gaze trailed from the septum ring to the blazing red mark at the center of her forehead.

The reflection didn't have Rel's curves. It was leaner, even with the weight of a pup.

"What are you?" Rel whispered to the reflection. She looked over to the Kalika. It seemed oblivious to Rel's musings as she carried on with her search.

Rel studied her reflection. She wasn't a Valravn or a Vulpii. The coloring was all wrong. Valravn were fearsome in appearance. Jet black hair with a white plume flowing at the center. Her mother told her stories about them from her traveling days. Rel flexed her hands. There were claws, but they didn't seem as intimidating as she imaged a Valravn's.

It could be a Vulpii from Clan Sky. Her mother taught of her about the varying clans. Those who thrived in snow-covered mountains, and those who thrived in warmer territories. Clan Sky possessed white fur, but she didn't think they had a euman form. Plus, their eyes were yellow or blue. The blood red orbs staring back at her were identical to her own. She'd never heard of a creature with such features outside of herself. Rel did not know what she was. She was lupine like the werewolves but not a werewolf.

"Who are you?" she asked her reflection, carefully turning to the side to examine her profile. The female staring back was bruised, a little haggard, but none of that diminished her beauty. Rel absently rubbed her belly. Affection swelled in her for the tiny life inside her. It didn't make sense.

The constant rotations over her belly soothed both her and the pup inside. The pup shifted toward her hand when it stilled. Rel snatched it away.

"What are you?" she asked the lump.

She's you," someone across from her said. It wasn't the raspy mewl of the Kalika.

Rel's head jerked up, eyes locking with the reflection before her. She was still in the dungeon's hall, but it had the look of a cave. Tendrils of dark smoke whipped around the sides of the mirror. It was no longer on the wall but hung suspended, cushioned by a frothy nest of gray smoke. Rel searched for the Kalika. She was gone, like the rest of the dungeon.

Rel watched, heart pounding, hands useless at her sides as the reflection bent forward and cooed to the unborn. Rel wished she could move away, but there was nowhere to go. The reflection straightened, resting its arms over its globus belly, then grinned at her.

"Ask your questions," it said.

Her mind filled with questions that refused to make their way to her tongue. She stared, and the reflection and it stared back.

"I am Argoel," it said. "And you," she pointed at her belly, "are this."

Rel's mouth moved, but nothing came out. Her head throbbed as she struggled to comprehend what Argoel said.

Argoel chuckled. It reminded her of the tiny chimes that hung from her window back home. When the breeze caught them, they sang their soothing song.

Rel looked down at the body she was in and compared it to the one in the mirror. They were identical, but inside, they were not.

"What happened to me?" Rel ran her arms along the length of her arms. The fairness of the strange skin was warm, though she expected it to be cool. "Why am I like this?"

"Why do you think?" Argoel prodded.

"I don't...I don't..." Rel paced, keeping a healthy distance between the mirror and herself. "I don't know!"

"The ways of the goddess are a mystery to us all," Argoel mused, she twisted gently from side to side, the heels of her hands pressed against her back. "Again, why are you here?"

Rel rubbed her belly as she paced. The pup inside shifted its position. She froze.

"Sihasin," Argoel cooed to her as if she were a pup. "Look at me, Sihasin."

Rel faced the mirror. "Don't call me that."

"Why not? It's what you are," Argoel said.

"I am not sihasin!" Rel thrust her arms toward the mirror. "I am not sihasin for the pack. I am not sihasin for my family," she said. Her voice rose as she thrust her arms toward the ceiling. "I am no one's sihasin!" Her growl ricocheted off the walls. "How can I be sihasin when I have none?" Rel's voice cracked as she dropped into a crouch.

Everyone wanted her to save them. She didn't get it. Her life existed within the boundaries of the land she shared with her family. When she returned, no, *if* she made it back, would there be a place for her? The alpha would kill or exile her. Her mother, who wasn't really her mother, didn't want her. And Grace! Rel wondered what secrets her adeeshí kept. Was she a denizen of the Deadlands? A minion of Gwyl?

"Sihasin. Sihasin." Argoel rubbed her belly as she looked intently at Rel. "Why are you here?"

"I don't know. I don't know. I don't know!" Rel answered honestly. "At first, all I wanted to do was save mother." Rel touched the face she wore. "I learned she's not my mother."

"A family is not about blood alone."

A weary grunt spilled from her as she shook her head. "Blood. Family! Pack!" Rel inhaled, hoping to chase away the rising frustration. It didn't help. Her head throbbed, and her shoulders ached from the burden she carried. "All this talk of pack. Family." She slapped her hands against her thighs and rolled her shoulders. "It's wearisome."

"It's the way of hope," Argoel said.

"Why am I everyone's hope?"

"It's why you were born." Argoel shrugged, then waved her arm toward the cells which materialized. The room shifted, allowing Rel a view of each cell. The abrupt move made her queasy, but she didn't throw up. The room retained its cave-like interior, but the cells were parallel to her, and they moved. Each cell slid by, pausing long enough for Rel to see the species inside and a sign mounted on the lintel. The signs identified the species and its abilities. After four of them drifted by, Rel caught the common theme: magic.

"I'm not magic."

Argoel laughed. The lightness of it made Rel feel safe.

"Things have been happening to you lately," Argoel said, stepping closer to the mirror's face, pressing her hand on the glass. Had the mirror moved with Argoel? It seemed closer.

"Sihasin."

Rel stared at her bare feet, her toes pressing the stone floor. She liked the tingle of light, air, and magic flowing from the mirror. If she stepped through...

"Sihasin!"

Rel flinched, refusing to look up. The horrors of the trials she endured added to the beauty of oblivion. If she disappeared, curse or no curse, her suffering would end.

"What happens to the Kalika, Sihasin? Or Viiya? Do you throw away their hope too?"

Rel stepped back. The cool air from the mirror was nice.

"Do you hate your life?" Argoel asked as she stepped out of the mirror.

Rel's heart stilled as the sheer image of Argoel approached. Rel's gaze ticked down, eyeing the path she trod. Argoel left no footprints.

"Do you regret the life you've lived?" Argoel stopped in front of her. The same tingle of light, air, and magic rolled along the tips of her toes. It hummed along her shin bone, forehead, and shoulders.

Rel didn't reply verbally or physically. She continued to stare at her feet.

"Do you hate the life Farah made for you?" Argoel lay her hand on Rel's shoulder, bending close enough for their noses to touch.

Rel shook her head as the faces of her family rolled through her mind. She would miss them even if she crossed over. She would miss them if she survived, and they didn't.

"Are the prisoners you left behind to blame for their condition?"

Rel's head jerked up, so her eyes were level with Argoel. "It's not their fault Ulmer's an evil bastard." Rel's words snapped like a whip. "He stole them! He hurt them." Her voice gained a growl. She felt the familiar prickle of her beast shifting about under her skin. "Why would I blame them?"

"You're ready to kill them," Argoel said. She gestured toward the mirror behind her. "Your death is a murder of hope, which would make you the spitting image of your alpha."

Rel bristled at the comparison. "You died!" Rel snapped at Argoel. "You died and left me behind. How are you better?"

Argoel stepped back and rubbed her belly. "I died for your sake. For your survival." She lay her hands on Rel's shoulders. "I died to plant the seeds of rebellion. A rebellion that's been brewing within the pack for years. I died to shed light on Ulmer's secrets." Argoel rocked side to side as she vigorously rubbed her belly. "Hope dies for a reason greater than ending one's own suffering."

Argoel pulled Rel into her embrace. "My death was a jiiq you to Ulmer."

Argoel's embrace tingled. Her skin smelled of dragon's breath and moon flowers. "How's that different from dying to end suffering?"

"A jiiq you to Ulmer is for the sake of all who suffer his leadership." Argoel's soothing voice siphoned from the despair coating her soul. "You are both a victory and the hammer of judgment to Ulmer."

Argoel pulled back from their embrace. "You, my beautiful daughter, are a goddess's design." Argoel grinned. "Luna doesn't abandon her people. Even the stubborn ones."

Argoel folded Rel into her cool, tingling embrace. Rel sank into it gladly. "Tell me, daughter, what will you be for your pack? Abandonment or a hammer of judgment to the one who preys upon them?

Rel squeezed her mother tightly. "A hammer," she said. Argoel's body dissolved into a spiraling ring of light. Rel passed through another door into a clearing.

Chapter 28
A God's Plan

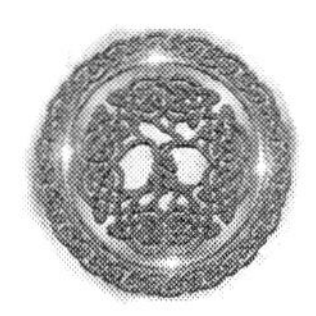

Gwyl examined his reflection. The neck was a mess with all the bruising and bits of bone peeking through it like extra teeth. He wrapped his hands around it. A brilliant green light flared from them. When he removed them, his throat was healed.

Gwyl twisted the head from side to side to test its mobility. It looked right. Gwyl didn't feel pain, but the soul still lingering in this shell could. Ho'yee was technically dead since he no longer had authority over his body. He couldn't wait to set Ho'yee loose for his hunt. There were many souls in the Deadlands waiting for their chance to do the same. His hunt would have to wait. The Eldritch Trials were in full swing, and the seeds of the rebellion were about to bear fruit. Gwyl would be there to collect his prize.

"Master, what do you want to do?" Grace asked, his eyes wide with questions.

"We will play a game while we wait," Gwyl replied.

Hearing his master use Ho'yee's voice was disturbing, but almost everything Gwyl did was disturbing.

"What game would you like to play?" Grace asked as Gwyl did an about face.

"You are going to watch over your mother," Gwyl said. He searched Blacktooth territory, sifting through the trees, the Commons, and Cubbies. His mind's eye glided through the territory, searching for Farah's signature. He grinned once he found her. She hid in a Cubby bordering Longtooth land. It wasn't far from the Arms of Luna.

"I am going to mingle among the pack," Gwyl walked the length of the hall, searching for something. He pressed against the walls as he moved, stopping once he found it.

"Come, Grace." Gwyl poured his magic into the wall. Loud pops reverberated, filling it. The floors vibrated. A large, narrow crack formed under Gwyl's palm. It spread, and the wall fell away, exposing a long red tunnel. Grace walked over to it.

"You know how to find her. Stay with her until Rel or I come."

Grace stepped into the red tunnel.

"She'll be scared," Grace said.

"Tell her she has no reason to be and that her sins were absolved a thousand times over."

Grace seemed satisfied with that answer, but still lingered.

"Ask me your question." Gwyl patted the dougan's shoulder.

"Can I be a girl again?" Grace asked shyly. "Being a boy is different, but I like being like Mother."

Gwyl chuckled. "We'll talk about that later. For now, your mother needs the strength this body provides." Gwyl squeezed Grace's bicep. "You can fight. With this body, you've got the power to properly protect her."

Grace stood a little taller.

"Now go. I'll find you when it's time."

"As you wish, Master." Grace gave a quick bow before dashing into the tunnel. Gwyl watched Grace until he vanished from sight, part of him dreading the talk they would have later. He couldn't change Grace back to a female. It was not something he could do.

Gwyl was a god of death. Drichians thought of him as a cruel and unfeeling god, but there was so much more to death than "the end." Death was a mercy for the suffering. He was a constant reminder to drichians that their time on Elderton had an expiration date. It kept most mindful of their deeds, while there were others who didn't care. The uncaring ones were the most fun on hunts.

Death was honest. It did not change for anyone. He stared down the now empty tunnel. Grace was a wonderful servant. Fulfilling his role as a familiar, he sent to keep watch over his chosen. Gwyl had many dougans that served as his eyes, ears, and, at times, hired muscle. They were wonderful creatures.

Smart, kind, and resourceful. Grace was the first of his flock to change genders. Gwyl was aware it was a talent among their kind, but none of the others had ever done it.

Once the trials were over, and he claimed his prize, he would sit down with Grace and confess to him his weakness. Though a god, Gwyl could not restore Grace's former gender, but what he knew of Farah, she would love Grace, boy or girl.

Gwyl released the portal, and the wall mended itself. He smacked his hands together, excited for the fun to come. He jogged out of the dungeons, exiting through the bulkhead doors. Clasping his hands behind him, he whistled as he strolled leisurely through the Fist. Hunts were the most thrilling when the hunter stalked his prey. He decided to start with the Hasking Stone Room. It was most likely where the alpha would be. If he was lucky, Ulmer would be there.

Chapter 29
What Makes a Monsters

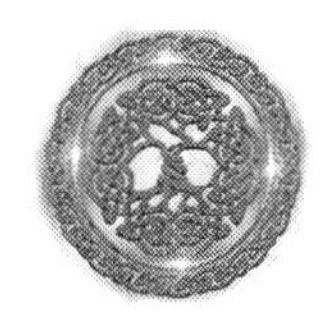

Running her hands down her body, Rel sighed, relieved that her physique was back to normal. Her hands lingered on her flat stomach. She absently rubbed it as she examined the clearing. She flexed her toes in the rich red-brown soil beneath her feet. Trees were spread apart, wide enough that she could see the jagged edge of a rock wall. It was too far to tell if it was a mountain or a hill. Rel looked up into the canopies that seem to stretch into the clouds. She needed to climb. Height would help her figure out her location. Knowing where she was would guide her next move.

All the running. The lives and memories of others beat on her skull and burned her skin. It wore on her. She circled the trees a few paces off the path. There were no branches low enough for her to reach. She would have to use her claws.

Rel wandered over to closest one and rubbed the trunk, savoring its texture and decided against it. The trees here were beautiful. With all the crazy she'd experienced, she wanted to enjoy the silence. The peace that thc Wilds provided. If only for a little while.

Brown trees dusted with moss formed a ring around the clearing. Roots knit through the soil, creating loops that could trip those unaware of them. Vibrant reddish-green ones were scattered among them. Some were a vibrant shade of reddish-brown that matched the soil. Deep green, blue and red leaves decorated the ground. She inhaled. Nuts, grass, fresh, unfettered soil were a welcome intoxication of nature. An errant breeze latched onto the scents and whisked them away carrying down the throat of the trails, flattening the tall grass and wildflowers which resurrected in its passing.

Birds chirped and something skittered off in the distance. Her nose flexed, sampling the world around her. There were libbits tucked in the grass. Another inhale, she detected a few Mgwans and something dead nearby. Her ears perked up. Wood crackled and popped. She smelled fire. She scanned the horizon for fleeing birds or dark billowing clouds and found none. It wasn't wild. Rel stood perfectly still. She waited for the wind to tell her where to go.

The wind fluttered about, tossing the ends of her half skirt. She inhaled again. The same wild fruit, grass and ripening dead streamed past. The dead thing wasn't far off. She wasn't curious or crazy enough to go and check on the dead thing. She tilted her head up, sampling the air drifting down from the east. A fire. She smelled fire. She headed east toward the scent of fire and burning wood.

The forest thickened the further she went. Her muscles burned, but life called to her in bouquets of wildflowers and fur. Maybe she'd find a Longtooth camp or the Lyew, Ayinda and Nicanor? Rel quickened her pace from a walk to a jog when she spotted what looked like fire up ahead. It wasn't wild. It was small. She would have missed it if she was looking up. Moving deeper into the dense woods, she crossed a small hill which, on her descent, it ended in a three-pronged trail where she stopped.

Trees lined all three with tall grass and wildflowers filling in the open spaces. Fallen leaves from the canopies overhead coated the ground, creating a colorful carpet. Rel found herself drawn to the trail littered with leaves the color of dried blood. A deep orange that glowed like embers in the sunlight. It was the path to her immediate right. The one on her left was covered with yellow and gold leaves, while the path ahead was black. At the furthest end of each path was a speck of flickering light. Rel tested the air in every direction and could only detect raw forest and a hint of decay.

There was something about the fire. Rel needed to reach the maker of that fire. She examined each path again, with her eyes and her nose returning to the same result. The surrounding trees and a decay tainted the trails. The flickering light at the end was mute. No scent or sound, only light.

Which way?

"It's safer in the Deadlands," a raspy whisper seeped through the leaves and descended from the canopy. It rolled down the trail in front of her. Firelight flickered on the leaves. Rel examined the trails, whirling wildly. The wind died along with any traces of fire, but the subtle scent of the dead lingered. At the end of each path, a light flickered. She squinted, her euman eyes weren't strong enough.

"Over here." The raspy whisper revived to her left. It rolled down the trunks onto the trails. A fresh squall stirred the yellow and gold leaves with its finger, drawing it up into a funnel. A guttural snicker danced with in the funnel. It tumbled into oblivion with the leaves once the squall settled.

Everything in Rel wanted to run away, but she had to get to the fire.

"Little wolf," the raspy whisper taunted. "Can you keep them safe when you return?" The raspy whisper curled along the shell of her ear, its tone scratching. Rel slapped at her ears, jerking her head left, right, then center? Searching.

A flash of white fur darted off to the side outside of her range of sight. It lingered within the shadowy fringes deep inside the trail. Leaves, the color of fire, tumbled across the ground. Rel didn't move. If she only moved her eyes, could she see the thing that whispered? If she saw it, would it lead her to the fire or would it, like everything she'd encountered, try to kill her?

Branches snapped to her right. Rel spun to face it, dropping into a defensive crouch as she searched the surrounding wilderness. Deep red leaves scattered by a sudden gust. She smelled it again. Decay. More pungent this time.

A familiar prickle flared beneath her skin followed by the sharpening of her sight. Narrowing her eyes, she looked deeper into the trail. Gaps between the trees tightened, forming a solid line. The red glow emanating from the fallen leaves was reminiscent of a throat. The trunks of the trees were like a lining, and the canopies above resembled the graceful curve of a neck.

Rel applied all her beast's senses as she paced the mouth of the trail. She couldn't smell anything. Hear anything and nothing moved. There were no signs of white fur. Her beast wanted to hunt for the thing with white fur, but Rel wouldn't let it. Danger was coming. She could feel it in her bones as she paced, considering her options of escape. She had to rely on her own speed and agility, hoping it would be enough to outpace her stalker.

Branches snapped on all four sides. An eruption of pale brown dust rolled across a deep orange carpet of leaves in her direction. It kicked up shards of wood and splinters that flashed like fangs. Her mind screamed at her to run. Her muscles were taut with readiness. She hesitated, as the other paths spewed splintered filled dust. She threw an arm across her nose, jerking her head forward, bringing her hood down. There was no time to tie her cloak. She braced herself for the pain to come.

Even with her nose covered, she could smell the ripening decay. It swished around in the converging dust clouds. Rel dropped to her knees, her cloak fanned out, giving her some protection as splinters rained down on her.

Something tapped her shoulder, the press of a body moving beside her. Crouching low, it whispered, "Over here."

Rel peeked through a tiny gap between her hood and arm. There! A flash of white fur and crimson. A wolf? Its ears were too long. It paced in worried circles a short distance away. In the haze, it looked like it walked on fire. It yipped. Rel crawled forward on all fours, shielded by her cloak.

It was an awkward procession, but as she continued, her stride became easier, more fluid as she trotted through the debris cloud. The white wolf yipped whenever Rel lost sight of it. It would dart out, as if by magic, close enough for her to see but far enough that she could not touch or smell it. The white wolf ran. Rel kept up.

Leaves crunched under her feet. It dulled as she and the white wolf move further away from the smoke-filled clearing. The further she got; the trail smoothed. Dust settled, giving Rel a better view of the white wolf. It was as big as a werewolf, but leaner. Its trot was graceful. Rel flicked her ears, noticing there was no sound accompanying the white wolf's movements. Every step Rel took, leaves crunched, yet the white wolf seemed to drift across them. The pads of its paws did not ruffle them. A quick glance at the ground. The white wolf left no prints.

The white wolf yipped and darted forward. Rel followed. It wolf led her through a tangle of bushes, through a path wide enough for its lean body to pass through. They emerged outside the gates of Elderton. The white wolf stopped along the shore. Hidden by the jumble of bushes growing from the water along the shore. It lay on its belly. Ears flexing. Rel crouched beside it. Her ears flexed. Wondering what it heard.

"Ah, the Unblemished Warrior," the goddess clapped her hands in delight. "Welcome to Elderton."

"Greetings, Luna," the wolf said, bowing low. Giving Rel a view of the goddess. She was different. She was statuesque, with gray skin and hair that seemed to blend into the night. It was done up in a braid that hung down her back. It swayed when she moved, like a pendulum. A silver band held the braid together. It winked in the moonlight. The face the goddess wore was not like the one Rel had seen. Elven ears framed a long angular face. There were no crimson orbs but glossy black pools with no pupils or irises.

The male bowed.

"Son, Chindi. I encourage you to keep the following questions in mind as you go through the trials. First, what is an alpha? What is an alpha to the pack? Finally, what is the pack to the alpha?"

Rel's head swam as the place where she lay shifted, moving in an arc until she lay on the docks. A large euman male dressed in the alpha's colors faced the open gate. Rel could not see the goddess, but her light outlined the male. The euman had waist length hair threaded with streaks of gray. He was as tall as her father Rafe and just as broad.

"Consider the trial won," Chindi said, flashing a cocky grin. "An alpha's born with the magic of the pack in his blood. To the pack, the alpha is law," he continued. "To me, the pack are my pups in need of guidance." Chindi pressed his hand to his chest. "A guidance that I provide."

Rel had never heard the voice before, but there was something familiar in the cadence of his words. The accent.

"My glory is their glory. As I aspire, so does the pack. We are not dogs to be dismissed and in time, my elevation to the council will bring the pack great honor."

"Ah, the Unblemished Warrior." The goddess clapped her hands in delight. "An honorable speech, but your house will prove your words."

The goddess walked backwards into Elderton, gesturing for Chindi to follow.

Chindi did not move.

"It is time," the goddess said. "Will you stand for your pack?"

Chindi scoffed at the goddess's words, his smile wavered. "I have led them for four hundred and thirty years. My pack thrives. They move among other species without issue."

"You mean when they are not fighting, stealing, or hiring themselves out as weapons of mass and minor destruction?"

Chindi looked away from the goddess, finding the ground interesting.

"Will you stand for the pack?" The goddess asked again. "Is it not the call of the alpha to risk your life?" The goddess arched a brow. "Shed a little blood for their sake." Her voice echoed in the stillness.

Chindi scoffed, "But is it not a test of the mind?"

The goddess laughed. Rel loved the sound of it.

"Will you stand for the pack?" the goddess repeated.

Chindi took a half step forward, rubbed his wrist, then stopped.

"I do not allow magical artifacts or devices inside the trials." She extended her hand, palm open, to receive whatever Chindi was hiding. "I only allow native magic. Magic born to species."

"I have no magical artifacts," Chindi huffed, taking a step back while cradling his left wrist.

The goddess pressed her thumb on Chindi's forehead. A loud pop followed by a rattle of chains. A dome of light flickered around him before it shattered into shards, then vanished. He hissed, shaking his right wrist vigorously as he jerked away from the goddess.

"No magic," the goddess said.

Chindi turned in circles as she searched the ground for traces of the magic's shimmering essence.

"I know this is hard for you being without your witch, but the trials are for you and you alone. Your mentor should have done a better job with briefing you."

The goddess grabbed Chindi's face, cradled it between her palms. "You've spent hundreds of years behind the barrier of your witch." Her hands slid away. "She's been your little secret, but she cannot help you. You are the champion." She waved an arm toward the path into Elderton as if presenting a prize. "Go and champion."

Brass squealed as pulleys and coils worked. The gate was closing. Chindi remained in the threshold watching the goddess.

Something moved across from Rel. Dark fur framed by moonlight prowled along the shore, then stopped. A werewolf lay on its belly, head pressed on its forepaws, in the undergrowth where the pier connected to land. Luminous green orbs tracked the exchange. Its ears flicked nervously.

As the gate closed, Chindi for a few moments longer before he did an about face. He jogged to the pier where a small boat awaited. He stooped to untie it, not bothering to spare look at them. The island trembled once the gate slammed shut.

Chindi clutched the left side of his face and screamed. Tendrils of smoke slipped through his fingers as he fell to his knees, never losing his grip on the boat's tether. He sank his claws in the wood as the rising smoke did not waver as he clawed the pier.

"The Blacktooth have forfeited their challenge. Cursed are you and your pack? For one-hundred years, both territory and species will be barren."

Chindi crawled toward the boat, tether in hand, and swung his legs over the edge of the pier.

"May your pack welcome you as you deserve. Alpha. Leader. Herder of your drichians." The goddess's words were steeped in disappointment.

Chindi hissed, rubbing his chest with the heel of his hand as he used his feet to pull the boat closer.

Outrage launched Rel onto her feet. A thousand curses found their way to her tongue as she stalked toward him. He ignored her approach as he did the goddess's words.

How could he proclaim his right as alpha when he pulled such a fatu move? She growled.

Chindi continued coaxing the boat closer. The tether in his hand hung loose. It wasn't secured to the boat. The knots had unraveled. Rel's walk became a trot as she closed the space between them.

The click of her claws amplified once she stepped onto the wooden pier. Another few steps and the sound of her claws multiplied. The pier shook under the weight of something big. Its weight caused the pier to shake forcing Rel to widen her stance before turning to see what approached.

A black wolf barreled down the pier toward Chindi. Toward her. It was bigger and faster than she expected which allowed her no time to move out of its path. Rel ducked, covering her head with her hands as she braced for the imminent collision. Wind from its passing body snapped her half skirt like a banner. She threw out an arm to keep from falling when she saw them. Tiny motes of light the same color as her skin drifted between her legs, fluttering like wisps. The motes settled on her skin which shimmered. Rel spread her arms wide and what she saw stole the breath from her lungs. Her body was as sheer as a worn curtain, yet it glowed like a star. The tips of her fingers itched to touch the radiant shimmering mass, but the smack of flesh colliding with flesh centered her. The light emanating from her ceased restoring her to flesh and bone.

Snapping teeth and scratching claws focused on her. Chindi and the black wolf were a tangle of flesh and fur. Blood splashing like water on the pier as Chindi did the work of staying alive as the wolf worked just as hard to kill him.

Rel didn't know if Chindi could shift, but she'd knew enough about shifting that if he did, the black wolf would end him. Chindi offered his arm as a sacrifice. It kept the black wolf's teeth from his neck. He used his other arm to push the wolf away, eventually adding a knee. Rel didn't know if she should disrupt the fight, but intervening felt better than doing nothing. Before she took a step, a hand grabbed her by the shoulder.

She looked up into the face of the goddess, or at least the face she wore. There was something familiar about it. Claws dragged along the pier, freeing a memory. The figurine she discovered when she first entered the house. Up close the armor looked like regular clothing. Rel touched it. Her gaze jerking up to gauge the goddess's mood. She touched without permission. With Rel, it usually didn't take that much to set her off.

The goddess nodded, lips curling in a gentle smile. Rel held up the fabric, noting threads of light swirling beneath the material. The light formed symbols. Rel pulled the fabric closer. Her beast sniffed it. Its way of discerning the good or evil of a thing, euman, or another wolf. It smelled of power. It smelled of steel and lightning. The scent nipped at its nose.

Rel looked at the goddess, studying her face. The harder she looked more of her mother's features surfaced. Longing drew Rel to touch, again, without permission, but the goddess didn't mind. Her hands traveled the contours, lingering at her chin. The outrage. The heartbreak. The sense of betrayal that tore her apart earlier vanished. She missed her mother. Worry resurrected, and she dropped her head in shame.

The goddess gripped Rel's shoulders gently, squeezing until she looked up.

"Families fight. Fights expose the root of sickness."

Rel looked over her shoulder at the fight between euman and wolf. "How is that helpful. One of them will die."

"It is the way of wolves," the goddess's voice turned Rel's attention back to her.

The goddess released Rel's shoulders. She took up one of Rel's hands and pressed it over her heart. "Werewolves are two natured. All species are two natured. Your natures have a physical form, but those natures are born from your heart." She tapped the back of Rel's hand with her finger. "It's your hearts that carry good and evil. There is no peace between the two, only dominance."

The goddess looked past Rel to the scene behind her. "Good and evil. The black wolf and the euman. Which do you think will win, daughter?"

The question surprised Rel, who turned around to watch bloody, snapping, and snarling bodies scrape for dominance. The black wolf with its fangs, claws, and feral need to control had an advantage. Its feral mind dulled pain. It was obsessed with its target. The black wolf with its fangs, claws, and feral need to control had an advantage. Its feral mind dulled pain and it would not stop until it caught its target. However, the human mind was vastly different. It held reason. It wasn't so rigid. It could adapt in the moment which gave it more options. A means to turn the tables of battle that didn't rely on its skin, teeth, and muscles. Putting down one's enemy didn't require a grand show of dominance. Like death, it didn't need to be grand. Death could be quiet and painless.

"I don't know," Rel said. "Either of them could win it." Her mouth slanted in uncertainty as the black wolf seemed to gain ground in the battle. Chindi spent most of the fight under the black wolf, offering his arms as a sacrifice to the wolf's teeth and jaws. A yelp severed the snapping, growling song. Chindi shoved the black wolf off him, pulling back a fully shifted forearm edged in sharp, thick black claws that were wet with blood.

The wolf whined as it limped away. Chindi shifted into his wehr form, which was outweighed the black wolf. The pier groaned under the weight of the two beasts. The black wolf rolled spun around, ears flat, fangs bared, and its tail arrow straight. It tucked its injured leg close to its body as its muscles coiled for another round.

"We should stop them," Rel said absently. She didn't want Chindi to die though her beast thought otherwise. There were too many questions that needed to be answered. First being, what the jiiq. He's alpha. His job is to do what was best for his wolves, not huff and puff and sing of his own glory. Secondly, she wanted to know who the black wolf was. She wanted to see it in its euman form.

Chindi looked up at her. His eyes hot embers scorching her skin. His lip curled revealing sharp teeth. An elongated jaw made his mouth look heavy. He snapped at her. The black wolf at his feet wheeled around and did the same.

Are you worried for our safety, little wolf. The black wolf's eyes ignited with blue light. They pulsed in sync with his words. The black wolf trotted forward. Laughter sparked in the air surrounding him.

Worry is for the weak. Chindi spat. His words, like the black wolf floated around him like a cloud. Wolves couldn't use their mouths in their wehr forms or while on four legs. Their teeth ate their words, leaving only snarls and barks. They spoke in their primal tongue. One that needed no euman language. Chindi flashed those too large teeth at Rel.

Mothers worry over their pups. Pups too weak to fend for themselves. They hover about like birds. Always searching for threats, but what can they do when the monsters come? Chindi stalked forward, falling in line with the black wolf. *Monsters need no protection.* He beat his chest, cutting it with his claws.

The black wolf chuckled as it limped forward. *The weak have no place in the pack.*

Chindi shook his head sharply. The blood from his injuries flew, landing in fat drops on the pier. *The weak have their place in the pack.* The gleam in his eyes was dagger sharp. *Fear sweetens the meat. Meat is the reward for the strong.*

The black wolf whipped his tongue around his blood-stained muzzle. *So sweet.*

Fear. Chindi and the black wolf said in unison. Their voices melded together, cutting at each other, breaking apart the word. It rattled.

Fear. So sweet. So tasty. Both wehr and wolf fell instep as the duality of their voices died, becoming a singular guttural tone. Chindi and the black wolf paused. The blood staining the pier rolled toward them. It spiraled around the pair as their bodies jerked and stretched. Two became one as the blood wrapped around their bodies. When it was done, the thing it became grinned at Rel with bold white teeth.

CHAPTER 30
ALPHA BARK

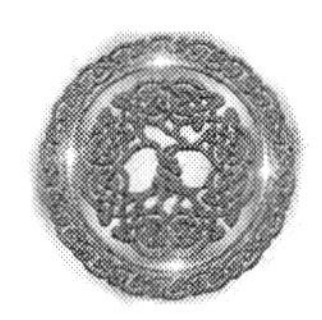

Mia glared at the assortment of grumpy males sharing the fire with her. They had the look of warriors, but she'd spent a few hours with them, and she had questions. Since she entered the camp, she noticed the males kept to the ground while the females and pups existed in the trees. Mia thought she was too old for envy, but she envied the subtle utopia over her head.

They strategically scattered tree houses built from the same wood as the trees hosting them. A layer of branches hid from plain view. The only reason she knew they were there was because she was told. The fire and magic lighting the insides mimicked the sun. Mia wanted a closer look. She suspected that some of the leafy branches were grafted on to provide more coverage.

Fire popped, resurrecting Mia's ire at her grandfather. He poked a stick into the fire. It was clear from his facial expressions that he was not interested in Rafe's message. The note Rafe sent with her lay crumpled and abandoned painfully close to the fire he tended.

Laughter drifted down from the surrounding canopies. She looked up at the warm glow of dragon's breath and magic, which lit the tree houses above them. The Longtooth had many homes, such as the ones overhead. Her grandfather told her as much as they walked from the clearing to their camp.

She couldn't help the jealousy rising inside her at the ease with which the pups played. They were free. Protected, unlike the pups in her pack. Mothers clung to their pups for as long as they could. Guarding them as they neared the age of *Choosing*. Some mothers would hide their pups, which earned them punishment. Every mother and her pups dreaded the day when a den mother accompanied by a trio of Fangs came to collect their sons. If there were daughters, the alpha would send for them later. When they reached an age of breeding.

Mia owned the truth of her ire as she glanced over at Ok'r. She wished he'd come for her when she was little. Saved her from Ulmer. The part of that truth that scorched her blood was his apathy. How could he stand by and watch the pack suffer, his family suffer?

A thump snapped Mia from her dark musings. She looked down at the spot where the object landed. It was a knife.

"I think a blade cuts better than a look." Ok'r groused. "At least you get the satisfaction of blood."

Several of the males chuckled while the rest ignored them.

"I'd be careful, Ok'r," a gray wolf said. Her grandfather introduced him as Gaun. Gaun was an average sized werewolf, but he had overlarge canines that extended down the sides of his mouth ending at his chin. Even in euman form, Guan's mouth seemed big, and his canines did not change. They added menace to his look, but his eyes were watchful and full of mischief. He jabbed an elbow in her grandfather's side. "It's better a female eviscerates you with a look. You can survive that," He chuckled.

Ok'r rolled his eyes, snatching up the crumpled ball of paper from the ground. He held it out for the others to see. "She wants us to bleed for this."

Guan cocked his head, eyebrow arching as he studied the tiny ball of paper. He cut his eyes at Rel.

"How'd you get a little piece of paper to aggravate your grandpa," he said, then fell over, laughing at his own joke.

"Asking for help annoys my grandfather. He can't be bothered with my pack's struggle to survive," Mia said. She felt her eyes roll as she spoke. "He's too busy living his best life to worry about another wolf."

"I've extended shelter to you and yours," Ok'r snapped. "As blood, I am honor bound to receive you."

Mia plucked up the blade and plunged the tip into the ground beside her and grunted. "Honor," her face puckered as if the word tasted bitter.

"Your alpha is the one who lacks honor," a growl layered Ok'r's speech. "He's perverted the way of the wolf.

"What about you?" Mia aimed the tip of the blade at her grandfather. "You've built this." She waved the blade at the canopies. "You've started new families, though you have families in the in the Commons. Wives, children, and grandchildren." Mia slammed the blade into the ground, sinking it to the hilt. "You play warrior." She gestured around the circle. "Fill the minds of your children with stories of glory." Mia leaned in, allowing her wolf to flow into her eyes and hands. She borrowed its claws and growls. She skewered them with her gaze. "How proud would your families be if they knew how cowardly you are?" Mia's lip curled, exposing the edges of her wolf's teeth as they cut through her gums.

Ok'r and three others launched to their feet. One shifted into a deep brown wolf. He charged and snapped his teeth near her face and retreated. Scars wrapped around his middle and there were more along his muzzle and along his flank. Those scars had no fur. Her grandfather glared down at her, using his height to cow her.

Mia met his eyes and said, "Where is the lie, oh great and mighty Longtooth? Pride of the alpha. The fang and claws of the Blacktooth." Mia rose to her feet. Her gaze meeting the eyes of all sitting at the fire. She flashed her teeth, and her wolf did the same. "You could have saved the pups. Come for the aged or the wounded."

"They would crawl back to Ulmer, on their bellies, with their tails between their legs the moment he called them back," Ok'r thundered.

All the laughter above them died.

"One of you could become the new alpha," Mia declared. "All of you have the skill and wisdom to lead." She assessed them with a glance. "Surely you can put him down in a fight."

"What of his Fangs," Guan said. "What of the wolves so broken that they would put themselves in harm's way to maintain what feels normal?"

"You've fought in wars. I'm sure you've won over your enemies." Mia stared into the fire. The wolves of her pack were broken. Even she couldn't deny the truth of Guan's words. "How do you handle your battle scars? The broken flee from the terrors that come from here." Mia pointed to her head. Her finger drifting down to her heart where it stayed. "And here? Do you treat them how you treat my pack? Your family?"

"Ulmer's pack, they're not warriors. They don't have the scars of war." Guan said.

"What Ulmer does is war." Mia looked around, daring them to challenge a truth they were determined to deny. "He preys on eumen he never trained to fight. He sets his Fangs on puppies." Mia paused, letting her words sink in among them. "He trees his blood like prey."

"To set upon Ulmer, some of us will die," Guan stated, then walked away from the fire. He didn't go far. He lingered under the long shadows of the tree.

"Isn't death something that happens to all of us," Mia said, holding her head high. "Mine is guaranteed, should I return."

"I know it is the belief that the old are ready to die," Ok'r said. "Just because I'm old don't mean I've made peace with death. I know death. I've crossed paths with it a few times in my life." He poked the fire. Stirred it, fixating on the tumbling stones which kept the fire alive. "I can't say I fear it. I respect it." He tossed the stick into the flames, leaning back against the tree flanking him. "I won't be angry or fearful of it when it finally comes to me." He held up the crumpled ball of paper between his thumb and forefinger and shook it at Mia.

"But what I will not do, is toss my life aside for a bunch of wolves who are just going to lie down and die after all the work I've put in to help them survive." There was a bite to Ok'r's words.

"Didn't you pledge an oath to Gwyl every time you walked away from a fight with your life?" Mia pressed. "How does it go again...

Second chance.Second life,May this vessel exist for sacrifice.I am honor bound to fight to preserve lifeAs penance for what I've taken."

Mia flicked her wrists toward the canopies, then to the lot around the fire. "You mock the broken, blaming their brokenness as the reason you refuse to help them." Mia laughed. It was full of bitterness. "How easy it is for the strong to prey on the weak."

Guan opened his mouth to protest, but Mia held up her hand and stopped him.

"Preying on the weak isn't always done with fangs and claws. It's being able to protect them. Preserve their lives for the many you've taken in the name of war. But you don't." Mia shook her head at them and walked off into the shadows.

The Longtooth sat in silence around the fire. Shame had their tongues.

Guan looked over at Ok'r and said, "I was wrong about giving a female a blade. At least you bleed out from a cut." He stepped into the light of the fire; arms folded across his chest. "Your granddaughter's tongue is way sharper than any blade or claw that's cut into my flesh."

"What say you, brother?" the gray wolf who charged Mia said. Her words shamed his wolf. It left him to chew on her words. A tall gray-haired male decorated with scars walked over and crouched by the fire. "It's been ages since we've been on a hunt."

"I swore I'd never go back to the Blacktooth until I heard my true alpha's call." Ok'r looked down the path Mia took. "I guess we'll be going sooner," Ok'r said and trotted down the path after her.

Rel couldn't move as she sized up the shiny black thing with the bold white teeth. Her heart knocked against her ribs as if it were trying to escape. Rel relaxed her limbs, prepping her body to fight or run. As she moved, she noticed the goddess was gone.

She glanced over at the place where she hid with the white wolf. The little collection of bushes was empty. Even the water had calmed. Not a wave. Not a breeze. Only stillness.

The shiny black thing breathed. It exhaled like a serpent. Rel expected a forked tongue to dart between those bold white teeth. Instead, it rocked. It watched her.

Mvunaji. The word floated around the shiny black thing with bold white teeth. The word started off harsh but dulled to a purr. *Who gave you that name?* It said, *It's not worthy of you.*

It took a step forward.

Rel took a step back. She used her peripheral vision to find he quickest route of escape. "I assume the pack," Rel said.

It laughed. *Mvunaji*. The word trembled in the air. *Mvunaji break souls to be devoured*. It took another step forward. *You do not.*

Rel took a step back. "I'm not a reaper. I am a daughter to my mother."

An alpha is Mvunaji. We reap. We tear. We devour. It said with pride as it stalked forward.

Rel did not retreat, but stood her ground. For too long, the pack had suffered under such a belief.

"You're wrong," she said.

The shiny black thing stepped forward. Its body reshaped itself into a wolfish creature with teeth bold and white.

"It takes a reaper to know the wounded and the dying." Rel took a step forward, squaring her shoulders. Making herself bigger. "It takes a healer to mend the wounds and restore the broken." Rel took another step forward. Something unfurled within her. A small flutter at the core of both her heart and mind.

The thing in front of her grinned, flashing its teeth, puffing out its big barrel chest, and looked her in the eye.

"You challenge us," it said.

Rel was growing tired of the games. Dominance Fights. Feral Runs. All games designed to cull weaker wolves.

Rel walked forward as the shiny black wolf moved to meet her.

"Only Mvunaji can be alpha," it said and charged.

Rel felt a snarl rise in her throat as she surged forward. The fluttering sensation in her heart and mind became a tingle that spread throughout her body. As she ran, she felt her body shift. When her feet hit the ground, they were paws covered in red fur.

It was time to end this. Time to kill the monsters. She set loose a howl as she bared her teeth at the monster before her.

A fissure flared behind the shiny black thing with bold white teeth. Rel launched herself at it, teeth bared and ready. She braced herself for impact, but instead of slamming into a monster, she passed through it into a swirling portal. When she landed, she was a human again.

Outside the island of Elderton, a crescendo of howls joined Rel's song.

Chapter 31
New Beginnings

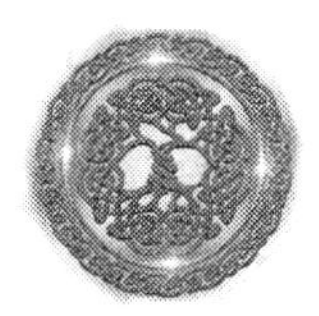

Rel landed on her feet in the hall of the House of Testing. The shadows were gone, and the lighting was warm and without menace. She strode through the hall, eager to find the door. Had she completed the challenge?

Her mind and heart were full and purpose clear as understanding took root. Her mother never imagined raising a child after a lifetime of war. Never had mother imagined hands that cursed and killed could shape a child. A child born of the Deadlands could be turned into a healer. Amused laughter filled the air as she passed through the modest living area of the House of Testing.

She shoved her hands in the pockets of her half skirt. Her fingers grazed something warm. She drew out a stone, like the one Rafe showed her. It was the Hasking Stone. It thrummed in her palm. She stopped, holding it out before her, marveling at the little stone that held so much power. The future of her drichians rested in the palm of her hands. Unlike the others who came before her, Rel knew what to do.

Rel thought that once she reached the front door, she would yank it open and run outside, but she didn't. Her heartbeat at the base of her throat. Once she opened that door, everything would change. The wolves would be hers to care for. Hers to mend.

Rel flexed her fingers on the cool knob. She inhaled, counted to ten and opened it. The steps seemed steeper than they were when she entered. Another deep breath. She could do this. Flexing her shoulders, she walked across the threshold and through a swirl of colorful lights. She stepped onto the porch and descended the steps.

The pack thrived under her grandfather Chindi's rule because he was focused on his glory. Chindi was fearless with his witch, her mother at his side. With his witch gone, he ran away from his greatest duty. Protecting the pack. Her father, Ulmer, was no better. Murdering his father to seize power for himself. His vision was built on his own cowardice. A mad wolf who savaged his own. He bred more like himself. Monsters. Ulmer needed to be put down. He needed to experience the terror he wrought.

Rel melted into her wolf. Her fur was a reversal of her patchwork skin. White in place of brown and brown where the white of her skin would be. Her ears, large with their red tips. They twitched as searched the ship and they sought out the waters of the Bijou. She took off running, reveling in the power building inside. The random orange discs that appeared in times of panic or need were gifts from her true mother. Cool tendrils of magic flowed from her core to settle in on her tongue. She threw back her head and howled as a portal appeared before her.

She was a culmination of well-laid plans and twisted vision. Rel set loose another howl as she slipped into the portal. A righteous anger quickened her run as the portal closed behind her severing her song.

Rel leapt from Elderton and ran parallel to the placid waters of the Deadlands before she stepped from the portal on the ledge of the Gorra Mountain overlooking the Alpha's Fist. Beyond it was the Commons.

"Welcome daughter," Ho'yee said.

Rel spun on him, teeth bared. Ho'yee sat with a knee tucked up to his chest. The other leg swung lazily over the ledge as he looked across the land beneath him.

Ho'yee threw a up hand up, gesturing for her to calm down. "Peace, daughter," he said as he looked at her. There was no white to Ho'yee's eyes but pure black with flashes of magic, jagged like lightning crawling where the irises should be. He grinned, teeth sharp and long. Ho'yee didn't smell like Ho'yee. He smelled dead. There was another scent there. She caught a whiff as she passed through the Deadlands. It held the bite of lightning coupled with the smell of night.

"All my pups recognize the scent of their master," Ho'yee said as he resumed his vigil over the land beneath him. "I am Gwyl," he said.

Rel calmed, taking her place at his side. Gwyl thumped Ho'yee's chest. His smile was feral. "This one is the first of many who I have come to collect," Gwyl said.

Rel noticed a flash of power dancing in eyes as he spoke.

Rel yipped.

"Join me then," Gwyl said, then snapped his fingers. Five orange discs appeared in the surrounding space. Five wolves, the same color as her birth mother, Argoel, stepped from them. "Join your uncles." The wolves bounced anxiously. "We hunt those who took my daughter from me." Gwyl's words crackled with power. He leapt to his feet. Spindles of magic whipped around his body. "We feast on monsters."

The surrounding wolves yipped, and she set loose a long malevolent howl. An obelisk of fiery light formed in front of Gwyl, who stepped inside. Rel followed him. One by one the Gwyl's wolves retreated into their discs. In seconds, the light of their magic flared, then vanished. Rel's howl lingered.

STAY TUNED FOR "WILD HUNT"!A FREE SHORT STORY AND EXTENDED CONCLUSION TO THE SONG OF SIN.

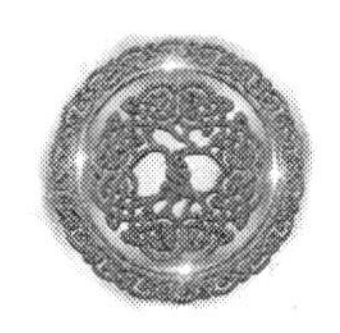

Enjoy this Book? Please Leave a Review!

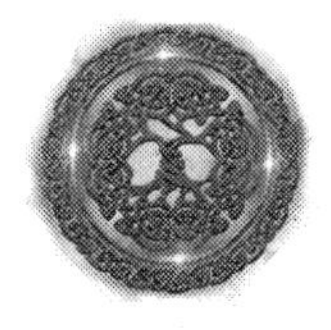

Reviews help authors in so many ways. Sharing your thoughts could help this book land in the hands of a new reader who may enjoy it just as much as you did. So please take a moment to drop a review. I'll love you forever!

Thanks!

Check out more of the Eldritch Trials

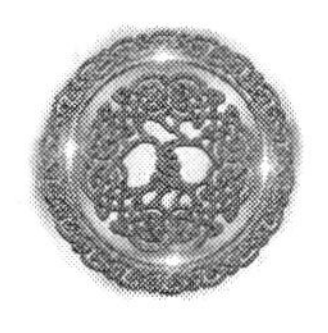

The Eldritch Trials is a collection of books in the same world, but each book is written by a different talented author! If you enjoyed this story, check out the others in the collection!
https://mybook.to/D8BymgW

About the Author

E. M. Lacey is an author who writes about diverse characters set in dark urban and dystopian landscapes. She's a coffee drinkin', meme postin', movie watchin' girl who loves to talk all things books and movies. You might bump into her at local comic cons and other such nerd fests. Whenever she's not getting her nerd on, she's writing, reading, binge-watching Netflix, or communing with horror movie fans and other authors online.

Ms. Lacey hails from Homestead, Florida but resides in Chicago, Illinois. She is working on her next piece.

Made in the USA
Las Vegas, NV
06 November 2023

80345474R00157